I0764358

THE TERMINAL PROJECT AND OTHER VOYAGES OF DISCOVERY

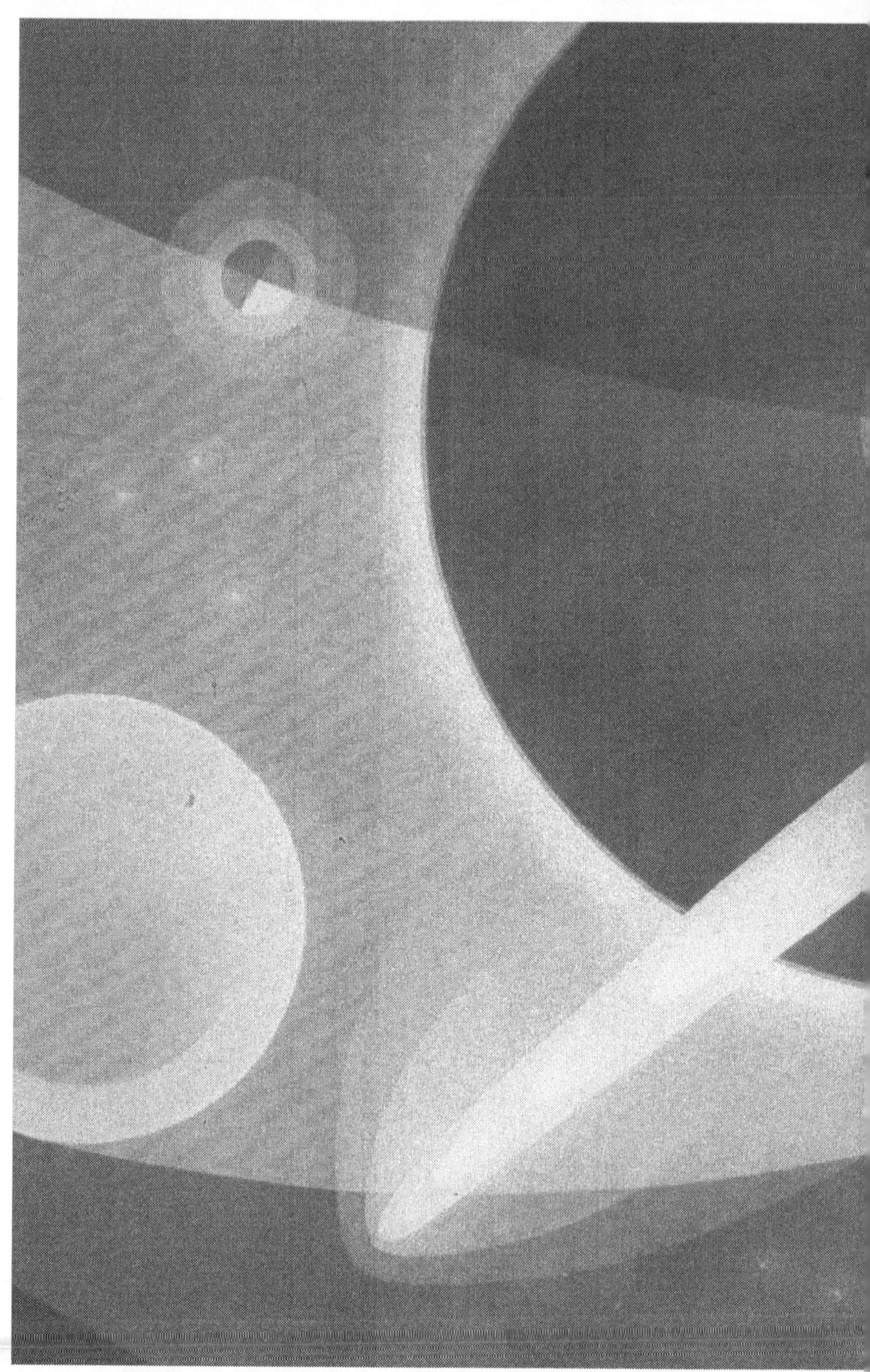

THE TERMINAL PROJECT AND OTHER VOYAGES OF DISCOVERY

Stories by

Melvyn Chase

SANTA FE

Sunstone books may be purchased for educational, business, or sales promotional use. For information please write: Special Markets Department, Sunstone Press, P.O. Box 2321, Santa Fe, New Mexico 87504-2321.

Library of Congress Cataloging-in-Publication Data:

Chase, Melvyn, 1938-
The terminal project and other voyages of discovery / by Melvyn Chase.
p. cm.
ISBN 0-86534-462-0 (alk. paper)
I. Title.

PS3603.H3794T47 2005
813'.54—dc22

2005012391

WWW.SUNSTONEPRESS.COM
SUNSTONE PRESS / POST OFFICE BOX 2321 / SANTA FE, NM 87504-2321 /USA
(505) 988-4418 / *ORDERS ONLY* (800) 243-5644 / FAX (505) 988-1025

To Paulette, the love of my life

CONTENTS

I

OTHER PLACES

THE PERIMETER

Tommy Harnett, TechSpec 5th Class, tried to stay calm. He took two or three deep breaths, and adjusted the focus on his Tri-D screen. The image of the oddly-shaped BEM ship moved slowly across the black backdrop of star-sprinkled space. And yes! It was coming closer, approaching the Perimeter.

Tommy smiled, nodded and thought, Come to poppa, baby. Come to poppa.

Tommy Harnett was not what you'd call a philosopher. So he didn't wonder why the war had started, or when it would end. He didn't care that the name of the enemy—the BEMs—was a two-centuries-old science-fiction joke. That it meant "Bug-Eyed-Monsters" in the days when space travel itself was possible only in science-fiction.

But Tommy *did* have a philosophy of sorts: Do unto your enemy before he does unto you.

That had always been his attitude, from schoolyard fights to barroom brawls. And now, after only four years in the Space Fleet, that same attitude had been rewarded with three rapid promotions and a chance to fly patrol duty on a BEM-catcher, the slang term for a one-man, mini-battle cruiser. (Despite its nickname, however, not one of these cruisers had ever caught a

BEM, or even *seen* one, for that matter, during the thirty long years of the war.)

Tommy zeroed in on the enemy ship and punched in its coordinates.

He thought, Now, I've got you. You're mine, baby, you're mine.

The Fleet had been on alert for three decades, its thousands of ships cradling the Solar System in a heavily-armed, protective, electronic net, scanning the space lanes, ready to attack and erase the enemy—an enemy that, thirty years ago, had boarded and destroyed a merchant vessel ferrying bauxite from Titan to the aluminum refinery on the Moon.

Only two men from the crew of that ship had managed to escape in a space-raft. They came back with the only eyewitness account of the BEMs—hideous, savage creatures, they said, who had tortured and murdered the rest of the crewmen. Our own Solar System was fully explored and fully settled, so the BEMs had to be intruders—invaders from some other star system.

The BEMs changed everything. Until their attack, the United Earth Directorate had been a world government in name only. Now the member nations were willing to give up some of their sovereignty—temporarily, of course—in order to combat a common enemy. They signed the Directorate's declaration of a global state of emergency and began to work together.

And they worked wonders. With contributions from scientists, engineers and factories all over the world, space-ship designs already in use were modified, altered, and improved. And then the Space Fleet was rapidly assembled, equipped, armed and manned. The shield was built. The war had begun—a cold war against a cruel enemy that could turn up the heat at any moment.

The Fleet's Tri-D screens stood guard at the Perimeter of the Solar System, watching day after day, year after year, catching sight of strangely shaped alien ships now and again—ships that almost always stayed in the interstellar no-man's-land, too far to reach, too near to ignore. Every now and then, there was an attack somewhere on the shield—but never in force. And there was never a breakthrough.

The Director General said, "They're searching for an opening, a weak spot. They haven't found it yet, but we can never let down our guard. *Never.*"

For the Fleet, the rules of engagement were simple:

Stay within the Perimeter.

Stay *out* of the no-man's-land beyond it.

Protect.

Defend.

Tommy didn't like those rules at all.

He said, "You don't win games on defense. We should go after them. We should bring it to them."

Of course, if he *did* go after them, he would be disobeying orders.

But that had never stopped Tommy before.

For almost six months now, he had patrolled his sector, criss-crossing back and forth, hugging the Perimeter, trying to be patient, watching his Tri-D screen, waiting, hoping. But until today, nothing. Just the icy, jet-black emptiness.

And then, there it was: the image of an alien ship. The enemy.

He knew that he should report the sighting to his commanding officer. That was Standard Operating Procedure.

But he knew what would happen if he followed S.O.P. Nothing. The BEM vessel would hover just beyond the Perimeter and then disappear back to wherever it came from. It would become another entry in the Fleet's log, with a note about time, place, and location, with Tommy's name, rank and serial number attached to it. And that would be that.

Not this time, Tommy thought. I'm gonna catch me a BEM.

That would make Mom and Dad proud. And it would surely stoke the fires in the deep blue eyes of Mary Mulcahy, Tommy's soon-to-be wife.

The alien ship was only a few thousand miles away. Its magnified image was strange and yet familiar, as if the BEMs had started building a human ship and redesigned it as the work progressed—almost as an afterthought.

For an hour or so, it continued to approach the Perimeter until it was only about five hundred miles away. And then, repeating a familiar pattern, it began to decelerate.

In a minute, Tommy thought, you're going to turn tail and run. That's what you guys always do. But this time, I'm changing the script.

Sure enough, it wasn't long before the BEM vessel began to turn its nose away from the Perimeter, until it was headed in the opposite direction. It started to accelerate, as expected. But, for the first time, a retreating alien ship wasn't alone. For the first time, an earth ship crossed the Perimeter and followed the enemy into interstellar space.

Tommy assumed that the BEMs knew they were being followed. Of course, he didn't know how fast their ship could go. His cruiser's fusion engine could push pretty hard. The enemy's science might be more advanced, but Tommy doubted it.

He thought, If they've got more firepower than us, or some other ace up their sleeves, we would have seen it by now. They wouldn't waste their time in a thirty-year stand-off, if they didn't *have* to.

The BEM accelerated. Tommy accelerated. The cat kept up with the mouse.

And this cat had a plan. He would get close enough to use his Rattler.

The Rattler was just off the assembly line. So far, only about half of the BEM-catchers were equipped with it. Tommy's was one of them.

The Rattler was like a tuning fork: it sent out vibrations. And it could operate in the vacuum of space because, like photons, the Rattler's vibrations were their own medium: they carried themselves.

At the high end of the range, the vibrations would tear apart a ship, a BEM and anything else that got in its way. At the low end, it wouldn't damage a ship at all but, assuming that BEM physiology was anything like humankind's, it would probably separate the alien from his senses for an hour or so.

There was no way to be sure of that, of course. Not until now. Tommy was about to perform the Rattler's first real-time field test.

He revved up his engine and shortened the distance between his cruiser and the BEM ship. The alien vessel speeded up and pulled away, but Tommy kept accelerating.

Even if the BEM's engine was a little better than Tommy's, the earth ship was much smaller than the enemy's, so Tommy could increase his speed more quickly. And he did.

The image of the BEM ship swelled on the Tri-D screen. It was only about a hundred miles away. That was approaching Rattler range.

Tommy gunned the engine again. Ninety-four miles.

And again. Eighty-nine miles.

Would the BEM turn and fight?

No, the enemy ship kept trying to escape.

Eighty-two miles.

Tommy armed the Rattler, punched in a low-range setting, aligned it with the BEM ship's coordinates and flight arc, and fired.

That's when he confirmed, first hand, why they called it the Rattler. The weapon had a kick—a reverse vibration that ran through Tommy's body like an invisible wave. His teeth rattled. His bones rattled. His consciousness rattled. Even his cruiser rattled. But just for a split second. Then it was over for him.

It was over for the BEM ship, too. The Rattler had apparently killed its engine.

Tommy caught up with the alien ship so quickly that he overran it. He decelerated and spun in closer. He activated the boarding tunnel, reached out with it and attached it to the hatch on the side of the enemy vessel.

He examined the ship carefully. It was about the size of a 7B6 frigate. In fact, its hull was exactly the same shape as the frigate's. But there were curved, lacy aluminum extensions fore and aft, and a series of small cylinders along the keel. Tommy couldn't even guess what their functions were.

With a mobile Tri-D camera, he studied the hatch. From the size and shape of the locking mechanism, it seemed to be designed for a space-gloved hand very much like his.

For some reason, that made him uneasy.

He shook off doubts.

He thought, I'd better nail them while they're still out cold. I hope they *are* out cold.

It took him virtually no time to seal himself into his space suit. He opened the hatch, pulled his weightless body through the boarding tunnel, hand over hand. He melted the enemy hatch-lock with a tight laser beam from his projector, opened the hatch and moved into the interior of the BEM ship, projector thrust in front of him.

It was dark. Maybe the BEMs didn't need light. Or maybe the Rattler had killed the power grid in the ship. It didn't matter; he switched on the light source in his helmet.

The corridors were neither too big nor too small for him. The BEMs must be about our size and shape. But where were they? And how many of them were on this vessel?

His helmet light illuminated a sign on a narrow door in the hall: "Code Red Gear."

Tommy stopped and stared at the words.

Code Red Gear?

There was a sudden tightness in his throat.

Tommy Harnett was a tough, aggressive, no-nonsense sailor. And this was nonsense: an alien vessel with a familiar Space-Fleet sign in it.

He forced himself to keep moving, almost automatically. The control room should be just ahead. The door was open. In a chair facing a bank of screens and dials, an unconscious figure was slumped over the instrument panel.

Tommy moved to its side. His helmet light illuminated the figure.

It was a thirty-year-old, crew-cut Space Fleet Lieutenant.

Tommy examined the instrument panel.

He thought, No wonder this looks like a 7B6 frigate. It is one. They just dressed it up to make it look like a BEM ship. But why?

Tommy found the power switches on the instrument panel and re-booted the system. The lights flickered on.

Tommy unlocked his helmet and took it off. He slipped out of his space suit.

The engine stretched and sighed and waited for orders.

Tommy watched the lieutenant and waited, too. He didn't waste time trying to solve the mystery. He'd let the "enemy" do that for him.

It was almost an hour later when the lieutenant began to regain consciousness. He raised his head slightly, turning it from side to side, moved his arms and legs, moaned and sat up.

Tommy pointed his projector at the officer and said, "Good morning, sir."

The lieutenant turned, worked hard to focus his eyes, and said, "Who the hell are you?"

"TechSpec Fifth Class Tommy Harnett. Perimeter Task Force Forty-four. And who might you be, sir?"

The lieutenant stood up and turned to face Tommy, who could now read his name-tag: "MORGAN."

Tommy added, "So you're Lieutenant Morgan. Is that a common BEM name?"

"You'd better put away that weapon, sailor. That's an order."

"Sorry, sir. No can do. I just chased down an enemy ship and it turns out to be one of our own frigates—with what appears to be a Fleet officer at the controls. I'm not making any decisions until I know what this is all about."

The lieutenant shook his head. "Don't be a fool, sailor. You're way out of your depth."

"Maybe so, but I've got the weapon and you're on the wrong end of it."

The lieutenant sat down. He shook his head again.

"You don't belong out here. You're not authorized to cross the Perimeter."

"But think of all the fun I would have missed, if I'd followed the rules."

"You're making a mistake."

"I'm also getting more and more impatient. Now, tell me what you're doing out here. And why you're pretending to be the enemy."

"I can't."

"Then, as far as I'm concerned, you're a prisoner of war. Hell, I don't even know if you really *are* a Fleet officer. I'm taking you and your ship back to the Perimeter. We'll give Fleet Intelligence a chance to talk to you. That's their job."

"We're not going back."

"That's not your decision."

The lieutenant seemed very relaxed.

"You're right about one thing, sailor. This is a frigate. And, as you may recall, a frigate is a *two*-man ship."

Tommy reacted almost instantly, crouching and pivoting in place, catching a glimpse of a sailor behind him. But Tommy wasn't quick enough. Before he could fire his projector, he felt the raw impact of a stunner, freezing his nerve endings and paralyzing his muscles.

A black curtain slammed shut over his eyes, and he fell headlong into that blackness.

Tommy awoke in a narrow, windowless and bare room. The walls and ceiling were gray. He was stretched on a cot in one corner. There was a steel door in the opposite wall. A thick, wooden table stood in the center of the room. Two wooden chairs faced each other across the table. A tiny camera watched him from its perch near the ceiling.

Tommy thought, This is a prison cell. Whose prison?

He didn't know how long he'd been unconscious. He stretched and sat up on the cot.

Then he walked to the door. There was no visible lock or handle on its smooth surface. It was cold to the touch.

He went over to the table and sat in the chair that faced the door.

He looked up at the camera and said, "I'm ready whenever you are."

There was no response. For half an hour, Tommy sat and waited for something to happen.

Finally, the door was unlocked and opened. Two men entered: a sailor, armed with a stunner; and Earth's Director General.

His was a very familiar face. He had been re-elected to office for more than thirty years—since before Tommy was born. Tommy had seen him many times on Tri-D broadcasts.

In person, he looked taller, slimmer, older.

The sailor closed the door behind him and pointed his stunner at Tommy.

The Director General walked over to the table and asked, "Would you like something to eat or drink?"

His voice was strong and resonant.

"No, thank you. I—I don't . . ."

The Director General smiled and asked, "May I join you?"

Tommy nodded.

The Director General sat down at the table and rested his hands on the bare surface. Although his face was lined and his hair was white, Tommy thought that his dark eyes seemed very young, and they were deeper than deep space.

The Director General said, "TechSpec Harnett—may I call you Tommy?"

"Yes."

"Tommy, I know you're confused. And I promise that I'm going to clear up the confusion. But I'm also going to ask you to perform a very difficult mission. And I pray that you'll agree to do what I ask."

Tommy didn't know what to say, so he just nodded.

"I've read your service record, so I'm not really surprised about what you did. I suppose, in retrospect, we would have been wiser not to assign you to solo duty on a BEM-catcher."

"Maybe I broke the rules, but I thought I was doing my job," Tommy said.

"I know. I understand."

"But wasn't I sent out there to catch BEMs?"

"No, Tommy. Catching BEMs wasn't your assignment. There are no BEMs. There is no alien invasion threatening us. There is no enemy. There never has been. There are only Earth ships masquerading as the enemy."

Tommy stood up.

"And the Fleet is just a bad joke?"

The sailor with the stunner moved forward a step.

The Director General raised his hand. "Please, Tommy, sit down. Hear me out."

Tommy sat down. He felt angry and, what was worse, he felt foolish.

The Director General said, "When I was elected the first time, more than thirty years ago, the United Earth Directorate was beginning to make progress. We were creating a more peaceful world. But the gains were slow, and every time we took two steps forward, a war would break out somewhere, and we'd go back one step. But there were some positive signs."

He leaned back, smiled and continued, "For example, there was a gradual, but steady decline in racial tension. And the reason for this was a very practical one: the continuing increase in interracial marriages. That began to melt the barriers between black and white and brown, and to dissolve bigotry and hatred. But we still needed time to move that process further along."

He gestured vaguely toward the sky. "We had begun to terraform Mars. And it was clear to us that, if we turned that planet into a granary for the Earth, we could not only ensure tremendous profits for agriculture, but also have enough surplus food to feed our whole world. That project was just beginning, and all we needed was time—to banish hunger, for the first time in human history."

He stopped for a moment, and then added, "We reached that goal, just a few years ago. Because we had enough time to recreate Mars, and plant our seeds, and reap our harvests."

He nodded and said, "Time. That was the magic ingredient for all of our plans. But would we have that time? How could we be sure that we wouldn't be stopped by that most fearful monster: *ourselves*."

He leaned across the table. "Do you really think that any alien race could do as much damage to us as we've done to ourselves? Endless centuries of war, cruelty, hatred, exploitation. Do you think that we had to find some Bug-Eyed-Monster out in space to threaten our survival? That monster, that threat, is in us. Perhaps we should hang a sign on the Perimeter that says 'BEM—Beware! Earth Men!'"

Tommy said, "So you made it all up."

"Yes. We made it all up. We invented an enemy. Because, when there is a common enemy, people work together and fight together until that enemy is defeated."

"You faked the first attack. And, every once in a while, you send a phony BEM ship in to remind us that we're not out of the woods yet. And the way you set up the rules of engagement for the Perimeter, no one could ever really get close to the BEMs."

"So far, there have only been a few wild cards like you in the deck."

"I'm not the first?"

"No, you're not. But you're the first in the Fleet."

Tommy looked over at the sailor with the stunner and said, "And what did you do to the others?"

"We told them the truth. We re-educated them."

"*Re-educated*. Is that a code word?"

The Director General smiled.

He said, "No, it isn't."

He leaned back in his chair, paused for a moment and said, "Tommy, we've made great progress over the last thirty years, and the 'threat' from the BEMs has been the key to it all. I'm a realist. I know that we still have a long, long way to go. So we still need that threat. Do you want to turn back the clock? Do you want to live in a world where we're fighting with each other, instead of banding together to fight a common enemy? Tommy, you took an oath to Protect and Defend our people. Did you mean it? Because, if you did, I'm asking you to live up to that oath. I'm asking you to *keep* fighting your war against the BEMs."

TechSpec 5th Class Tommy Harnett was not what you'd call a philosopher. But he *did* have a new philosophy of sorts.

Raising one clenched fist, he said, "Just let me at those bastards!"

LEAPERS

The future used to be years. Now, it's minutes—I don't know how many.

I can already feel the erosion at the edges of my mind.

I can already hear hundreds of voices, some human, some not, calling to me from the shadows, angrily, fiercely, echoing like the roar of a distant ocean that keeps creeping closer with every wave.

I can't hold on for long. I want to be one of those voices.

And there's another urge in me, too—a powerful undertow, almost a hunger, but it's still unclear.

A few weeks ago, this was just an adventure.

My friend, Tony Ackerman, called and asked, "How would you like to come with me on one of my bring-'em-back-alive expeditions?"

"Why would I want to do that? Sleep in a tent? Fight off snakes and tse-tse flies? Hack through the underbrush with my trusty machete? In your dreams."

Tony is—was—a zoologist. He lived in Manhattan, but most of his life was spent in remote, uncivilized, uncomfortable places, tracking down animals that only a zoologist could love.

"Jack, you've got me all wrong," Tony said. "First of all, we're not going to the jungle."

"What do you mean, 'we'?"

"Jack, you could actually be there when I discover a new species. A new species."

"Why don't you just tell me about it when you get back?"

He paused for effect, then said, "This could be the cure for your writer's block."

"I don't have writer's block."

"So how come I haven't seen any articles with your byline for—how long has it been?"

"I'm working on my book."

"Sure you are."

Tony was right. I was stuck. I wrote every day, from eight in the morning until noon, the way I always did. But suddenly, I couldn't find my voice. When I tried to be sophisticated, I sounded cynical. When I tried to be warm, I sounded pathetic. When I tried to be analytical, I sounded cold.

I said, "The jungle is not the answer."

He laughed.

He said, "I told you: we're not talking jungle."

"What are we talking?"

"Picture a peaceful, temperate valley in the Andes Mountains in Chile—a valley that has been isolated for centuries by sheer, icy cliffs—a pocket of life trapped in a deep, rocky gorge. Then, suddenly, the earth shifts, and an avalanche opens a door to that valley. You may have read about this, a couple of weeks ago."

"*Earthquakes? Avalanches?* In that 'peaceful, temperate valley'? Any volcanic eruptions I should know about?"

"Listen, Jack. It'll be like a hike through the mountains. And the valley is a dream world for a zoologist. Almost untouched. Like the Garden of Eden before the Fall."

"And some august institution is willing to finance your trip to Paradise?"

"That's right."

"Who? Harvard? The American Museum of Natural History? The National Geographic Society?"

"Actually—my mother."

I groaned. "I hate rich kids."

"If I wait until the big outfits start sending people down there—even if one of them sends *me*—there'll be too many cooks. I want to get there before the stampede. I have to. And I want to tell the world about what it was like to walk in forests that no human beings had seen for centuries. I want to share the excitement of finding new forms of life—new evolutionary pathways."

"If there are any."

"Trust me. There will be. I feel it in my bones. But I don't have the talent to put the experience into words. You do. I'll bring back the animals. You bring back the story."

"What if we discover a new form of mountain lion?"

"Jack, we're not going out there alone. We'll have five or six guys with guns, just to protect *you*."

I waffled for a while, but Tony was right. I needed something to jumpstart my writing.

So I agreed.

That was three weeks ago.

The voices are louder now. I can feel them pulling me toward them. And the other hunger is getting stronger, too.

I have to remember. As long as I can remember, I can be Jack.

We flew down to Santiago and chartered a shabby, single-engine propeller plane that looked like World War II surplus.

By this time, there were six of us on the expedition. Tony, who taught at Columbia University, had hired one of his graduate students, Eric Ramirez, as a second-in-command who could also serve as our interpreter. A botanist named Kruger (a friend of Tony's from the Columbia faculty) and two local guides made up the rest of the crew.

I asked Tony when my personal bodyguard ("five or six guys with guns") would join us, but he just laughed.

We traveled into the interior in two all-terrain vehicles that looked like miniature tanks, with wide tracks instead of tires. They seemed to be able to climb over virtually anything, until we reached the narrow entrance to the newly discovered valley. We set up a base camp on the rim of a steep cliff, where we pitched our tents. From this point on, we had to proceed on foot.

We may not have been in the Garden of Eden, but the valley was beautiful. The cold, mountain air was clean and clear. In the cloudless sky, huge birds of prey soared in great circles on currents of wind, wings outstretched, unmoving, held aloft by invisible fingers.

There were few trees at the camp site, but below us the valley was thick with vegetation. And, hopefully, with animal life.

That night, I started to write. I hadn't brought my laptop. This was an expedition, and I thought it should be chronicled the old-fashioned way: in handwritten notebooks. (I hope to God someone finds them soon enough.)

As Tony had predicted, the words flowed easily.

He said, "I told you so. I knew this was what you needed."

He and Kruger set up a work schedule that started with short treks into the valley, with a return to the base camp on the same day. But navigating the steep mountain pass took too long to allow for much exploration, so they began to camp for a few days down below. Tony would always take me and Eric with him, and one of the guides. On those days, Kruger would stay at the base camp with the other guide.

When Kruger went out, Eric would usually accompany him, along with the other guide. Whoever remained in camp had time to write up his notes, analyze specimens, and prepare for his next trek into the valley.

At first, Kruger seemed to hit pay dirt every time he went out. He kept finding new varieties of vegetation. As a city boy, I didn't know one plant from another, but I tried to share his excitement.

At first, Tony was less successful. There were no immediate surprises. But it wasn't just a question of whether he would discover something new. On our third excursion into the valley, he told me how surprised he was that we encountered so few animals.

He said, "With the range of plant life, and the moderate temperature, there should be more animals and insects here. Where the hell are they?"

"Maybe it's that new species of mountain lion," I said, half-seriously.

He shook his head.

"No, Jack. Not unless there's some kind of predator that attacks everything from butterflies to frogs—to snakes, birds and field mice."

"Maybe there's a virus that developed here—that kills off most of them."

"Maybe."

He caught some grasshoppers, a speckled lizard, and a small, brown bird that looked like a sparrow. They seemed to be healthy. He dissected them, tested their tissues, and all of the fluids in them, and turned up nothing unusual, nothing deadly.

Then we found our first fresh corpse.

The voices, the shrieking voices.

The hunger.

A new way to live.

A new kind of death.

Don't listen, Jack. Don't *listen*.

It was a dead field mouse. Freshly dead, its dark eyes open, staring.

Tony held the tiny body in his gloved hand. He examined it with a magnifying glass.

He said, "No apparent wounds. No blood. It seems well fed. No broken bones."

"Maybe you'll find that virus now."

He carefully placed the body in a sterile sac, sealed it, put it in his backpack.

A half hour later, I found the body of a tree frog, draped over a low limb, freshly dead, still moist, seemingly uninjured.

It joined the field mouse, in its own sterile sac.

We stopped looking for living animals and began searching for dead ones.

We found one more fresh "kill": a slim, black snake, half-buried in the soil. (We had already begun to think of the dead as *victims*.)

At the base camp, Tony spent two days analyzing the bodies.

When he was finished, he said, "There was nothing wrong with any of them. They weren't diseased. They weren't injured. Their organs were completely intact. They were just dead."

"And you don't know why?"

"I haven't got a clue."

"I guess this Garden of Eden has a snake of its own."

He nodded and said, "We'd better find it. That earthquake opened the Garden gate."

I recognize one of the voices now. It's louder, clearer than the others. A human voice. *His* voice. I can almost understand what he's saying.

I can hear his pain. His hunger.

I can feel his pain. His hunger.

Jack is dissolving.

Not yet. Not yet.

Then we saw the leapers. That's what Tony called them.

There were three of them, perched on the branches of a tree. They were small, dark, furry animals—maybe a foot-and-a-half long, with a tail that added another seven or eight inches to their length. At first I thought that they were monkeys, but their faces were longer, with pointed snouts and very large, intelligent eyes.

They watched us intently. They had never seen anything like us before.

Tony said, "They're in the lemur family. Primates, but not as smart as us."

"They're probably saying the same thing about you and me."

They were chattering softly to each other, standing on their hind legs. Then, incredibly, with seemingly little effort, one of them leaped to another tree, thirty or forty feet away from his companions. A moment later they joined him.

Tony smiled.

He said, "They're not lemurs. They're leapers. Kruger, eat your heart out. No one has seen one of these before. I'll bet the farm on it. This one's going to be named after me."

"If you can catch the son-of-a-bitch."

Tony had already snapped some photographs of the trio.

He said, "We'll set a trap. Lemurs are omnivorous. Like us. They eat fruit, insects, small animals."

"I don't eat insects."

"You eat snails. That's worse."

We were both excited about the find. For the moment, we forgot about the snake in the Garden of Eden.

We set the trap later that day. We put a live lizard in it.

When we went back in the morning, the lizard was still there. It wasn't injured, or wounded. It was dead.

One of the leapers was sitting on a branch near the trap. Its huge eyes watched us curiously, fearlessly.

We set the trap again, this time with a live frog and some fruit.

When we returned to the trap the next day, the fruit was untouched. The frog was unhurt. And it was dead.

Two leapers loitered in a tree across the clearing. They chattered, preened, and watched us intently.

Tony was trying to unscramble the puzzle.

He said, "The bait is dying, the way those other animals died. And the leapers don't seem interested in meat, or fruit."

"You're only assuming that they have the same diet as lemurs. They may have evolved differently here. Maybe they just eat a certain kind of leaves. Or one particular insect."

"Maybe. So far, we haven't seen them eat *anything*."

We went back to the base camp, so Kruger could take his turn in the forest. He went out with Eric and one of the guides.

But Kruger didn't come back on schedule. We decided that he may have lost track of time, so we waited an extra day.

In the middle of the night, we were awakened by the sound of Eric's voice, half shouting, half moaning. He was crouched by the campfire, staring at the flames. Tony and I tried to talk to him, to calm him, but he just kept moaning wordlessly, his eyes empty and, at the same time, glazed with fear.

We carried him toward his tent and he went limp in our arms. In a moment, he was dead.

Tony examined him carefully. He was uninjured, except for some scratches from the underbrush.

Not yet, Tony. Not yet. Give me another minute. Another *five* minutes.
Yes, I'm hungry, too.
Soon. Very soon.

In the morning, we went into the valley to search for Kruger and the guide who was with him. We left the other guide at the base camp.

We found both of them, Kruger and the guide, unhurt, dead, in a shady grove near a fast-flowing stream of water.

We heard the chattering in the trees. We saw the dark furry bodies leaping from branch to branch. We looked up into those dark, dark eyes.

We ran back to the base camp.

In my journal, I wrote what Tony said.

"I'm sure it's them—the leapers. They're the predators."

"But they're not eating their prey."

"Evolution is a tricky bastard. Something special happened here. Who knows why? The leaper became a different kind of predator. It feeds on the *mind* of its prey—absorbs the prey's consciousness, turns it into flesh and bone and blood. And the body is left untouched."

"That's crazy, Tony."

"The leaper steals your soul—drains the energy from it—and packs it away with the hundreds of other souls it has stolen. Bird souls and insect souls and lizard souls."

He paused, and added, "What if it takes its prey's knowledge, too? What if its mind is the sum of all the minds it feeds on?"

"Tony . . ."

"Just think of it, Jack. The leapers have just discovered a new prey, a smarter prey, one that will make *them* smarter, too. All the things that Kruger knew—that Eric knew—that the guide knew—*they* know. They know about the world outside the valley. And all the fresh prey that is out here."

He put his hand on my arm and said, "We've got to find a way to stop them from getting out."

We were sitting in front of the main tent, where Tony and Kruger had set up their laboratory. Tony's eyes suddenly looked past me at a spot high in the air. I turned and followed his line of sight.

The leapers had left the valley. A crowd of them were gathered in the trees on one side of the camp. The guide sensed danger. He clicked a cartridge into his rifle and took aim at one of them. He fired. The leaper was hurled from its perch by the impact of the bullet.

In an instant, another leaper had launched itself onto the guide's back and clutched him with its tiny hands. The guide collapsed without a sound. The leaper looked at me and Tony.

It chattered a soothing, sultry song. And then all we could hear was that chattering, all around us, and all we could feel was the hot breath of oblivion.

I'm ready now. I'm one of you, all of you.
My voice is your voice. No more Jack. No more Tony.
We are stronger. We are smarter.
And we are free.
The gate is open.
We are hungry.
And there's a great, big world out there, just waiting for us.

BROTHERS

From the time he was a child, Emery Harmon had felt it: loneliness. Perhaps it was because his father had died before he was born. Emery knew him only from poorly-shot videos of family parties and from holograms in his mother's albums—living images of the dead.

Perhaps it was because, after his father died, Emery's mother withdrew from her family and friends. And she withdrew from *him*, too: feeding him, clothing him, but enclosing him in a wall of silence. She, too, became a living image of the dead.

Perhaps it was because he had no brother or sister.

Whatever the cause, Emery was unable to form friendships. He was unable to fall in love.

He was always lonely.

As he grew older, he transformed his personal loneliness into a cosmic yearning.

"We can't be alone in the universe. There must be life—intelligent life—on other planets. And wherever they are, no matter how different they may look, no matter how strange, they will be our brothers. And I want to *find* our brothers."

His loneliness had become a cause.

Fortunately for him, he lived at a time when that cause could become a profession: when Emery was ten years old, Charles David Lindstrom invented Laser Channeling—in effect, a faster-than-light drive. At last, it was possible to travel to the stars. (For some reason, relativity theory didn't apply: time in a Laser Channel didn't slow down. So if a traveler was gone for ten *ship* years, he would return ten *Earth* years later.)

The Solar System had already been thoroughly explored. All of the planets and satellites were barren. Except for Mars, where fossilized shells were found far beneath the surface—the three-billion-year-old remains of organic (that is, carbon-based), probably aquatic life.

But only the remains. There may have been soft-bodied creatures, too, but they left no clues behind them.

There were no artifacts on Mars—no indications that there was intelligent life that *knew* it was life—that had built something—created something.

Some scientists believed that life began on Mars and somehow migrated to Earth.

Emery didn't agree.

"Wherever—whenever—the conditions are right, life is a possibility. Those conditions may have occurred thousands of times—millions of times."

Emery prepared himself for the search. In college, he majored in biology, with a minor in chemistry.

He excelled.

He also followed a rigid program of physical conditioning.

By the time he graduated, he was mentally and physically ready to pass the rigorous exams for DeepSpEx—the Deep Space Exploration Project.

DeepSpEx accepted only five recruits a year. After eighteen months of Phase One training and conditioning, one of the five would be selected for Phase Two—six months of pre-flight prep. Many recruits washed out.

Even among the survivors, only a handful would ever actually become Explorers. There were several reasons for this.

First, although Laser Channeling (L.C., or Elsie, as it was called) had been invented more than a decade ago, it was a treacherous technology, difficult to harness, difficult to package, difficult to handle. Witness the deaths of the first three Explorers.

Moreover, building an Elsie engine, and housing it safely in a complex, crystalline alloy of aluminum, titanium and lead, was an enormously expensive undertaking—so expensive that the Elsie Ships were built as small, one-person vessels. This resulted in a whole new set of problems—emotional problems. An Explorer would be alone in the vastness of deep space, thousands of light years from home, on a dangerous voyage that could last for five or six years. Could he or she stand the loneliness?

Emery could. And he proved it to the psychiatrists who examined him. That was one reason he was selected to fly DeepSpEx XII.

Nonetheless, as added insurance against loneliness, DeepSpEx XII was the first ship equipped with a "Companion"—a brand new, one-of-a-kind android assistant that packed all its remarkably sophisticated neuro-circuitry into a minimum of space: it was the size of an eight-year-old boy, although it had the proportions of a miniature adult.

The Companion was designed to perform a variety of essential tasks: it could handle many of the technical functions on board; it was a self-repairing, indestructible, mobile array of life-sensing devices that could accompany the Explorer onto the surface of a planet; and, according to its inventors, it could also carry on a pleasant conversation.

Although he told the Program Chief that he didn't need a Companion, Emery didn't raise any serious objections: the only thing that mattered to him was to begin the journey that he had hoped for, and planned for, all of his life.

In fact, he soon discovered the value of his Companion: it was programmed with all the parameters of the voyage, the sequence of stars he would visit, the Elsie coordinates to reach them, and the documentation that would be required. These instructions were duplicated in the ship's memory, but the Companion would free Emery from all the routine, boring jobs aboard ship.

He began to feel a little friendlier toward the Companion. He even gave it a name. He picked "Christopher," short for "Christopher Columbus."

A week before the launch, Emery spent several hours alone with Christopher, going over the details of the flight plan again, and reviewing the available information about each star they would visit.

The little android's voice was incongruously deep and masculine and, for some reason, Emery mentioned that fact to Christopher. He regretted it immediately.

"Would you like me to change it?" Christopher asked. "Just say the word."

"No, it's okay. I don't really care what you sound like. I don't intend to talk to you very much."

"Don't be so sure," Christopher said, in a smug voice.

The android's expression reflected that smugness.

Emery smiled. "That's a little aggressive for a Companion, isn't it?"

"Not really. I wasn't programmed to be a yes-man."

Emery shrugged.

He said, "Well, I wasn't programmed to need much conversation. I'm used to being alone."

"But you've never been out there. You've never seen the blackness, the unblinking brightness of the stars, the cold emptiness. You've never been *that* alone."

"Neither have you."

"But I've been programmed with the images of past flights. Believe me, you'll be grateful that I'm out there with you."

"Maybe."

"Do you want me to show you how Elsie will make you feel?"

"How could you do that?"

"One of my sensors can detect telepathic imagery. Just in case we run into a telepathic life form. That's supposed to be all the sensor can do. But I've been playing around with it, and I've discovered that it can also *project* imagery."

"Do you mean that you can do things you're not designed to do?"

"Neural programming is an art, not a science. Who knows what other hidden talents I may have."

Emery felt uneasy. Christopher was a brand new model—a prototype. Maybe it hadn't been thoroughly tested. Maybe the little son of a bitch would go berserk out in space and . . .

Emery was willing to take a chance on that. He wouldn't delay his departure for anything.

He said, "I'll find out what Elsie is like soon enough. Let's talk about the odds."

"The odds?"

"You have the data from all the previous flights?"

"From the first six of them. Not counting the ones that failed. The others haven't returned yet."

"How many planets were explored?"

"You know the number already. Two thousand five."

"Just checking. How many planets did we actually land on?"

"You should know that, too. Nine."

"Only nine?"

"Only nine."

"And they were deserts."

"Deserts."

What if he spent the next four or five years searching—and came back with nothing? It wasn't just a matter of *where* he went, but of *when*: he could arrive before life evolved. Or after it had disappeared.

Deserts.

What if the whole universe were a desert?

What if we searched for a thousand years and never found our brothers?

What if life were just a bizarre accident in one tiny corner of eternity, never repeated, never duplicated?

Emery felt an icy wave of loneliness wash over him.

He shook his head. He wouldn't fail.

Elsie was a gentle name for an awful experience.

Emery had read about the process, so he knew that it had something to do with transforming matter into photons—particles of light—then back again to matter at the destination.

But how could light travel *faster* than light?

He didn't have the mathematical background to really understand Lindstrom's work.

After his first Elsie jump, however, one thing was clear: it wasn't the kind of thing you'd do if you didn't *have* to do it.

He felt as if his body had melted, or disintegrated, or exploded. He felt as if he were standing next to himself and inside of himself. He felt frozen in a block of ice and burning in a sheet of flame. And then he felt, for one long terrifying moment, as if he didn't exist any more.

Right after the jump, Christopher said, "You should have let me preview it for you."

Emery laughed. "I might have quit the program!"

When he looked at the image on the main video screen, he stopped thinking about Elsie. DeepSpEx XII was now a new, tiny asteroid in the first star system that he would explore.

Christopher said, "The name of this star is Procyon B."

"It's about the size of our Sun. A comfortable star, right in the middle of the Main Sequence—young enough and old enough. Are there planets orbiting it?"

Christopher inserted his left index finger into a socket on the instrument panel, connecting the ship's sensors to his processors. He began the readout.

"Yes. There are six planets in the system. We are just beyond the orbit of the sixth planet."

"Our first star—and it has a family!"

Christopher's deep, baritone voice cut through his enthusiasm. "Planet Number Six. Dead. Always was. Primarily frozen methane."

They were about two billion miles from Procyon B—a *safe* distance. According to Lindstrom's equations, if a ship jumping at full Elsie power came any closer than that to a star, the photons would never become matter again. The vessel, and everything in it, would disappear in a burst of light.

From now on, DeepSpEx XII could only take low-powered, short Elsie jumps. And when the ship came within two million miles of a planet, it had to switch to its standard, relatively slow, laser-thrust engine. That was why the Explorers' expeditions took so long to complete.

They left the sixth planet and focused on the fifth. A short Elsie jump—which was just as nauseating as a long one—brought them closer to it. Then Christopher activated the laser-thrust engine. The trip to Planet Number Five would take five days.

To maintain an Explorer's biological clock, DeepSpEx XII was calibrated to mimic an Earth cycle of nights and days. Emery's work period was ten hours long. At the end of each ten-hour span, the ship's lights dimmed for an eight-hour sleep period. When Emery woke up, he exercised for an hour: the ship's Drummond Screen generated artificial gravity that helped keep his muscles healthy. And if Christopher kept out of the way, there was just enough room in the cabin for sit-ups, push-ups, *et al.*

If Emery started feeling the effects of cabin fever, he had another exercise option: EVA—Extra-Vehicular Activity, which Explorers called A Walk on the Wild Side. He could put on his pressure suit, step into the airlock and take a stroll in space. The Drummond Screen generated a gravity field on the outer shell of the ship, too, so EVAs were perfectly safe.

During the six-hour post-sleep period, Emery could read (on the video screen) or watch a movie or listen to music or write an entry in his Log.

His food and the atmosphere of the ship were manufactured from a combination of his recycled wastes and a compressed plasma of molecules packed in a platinum alloy container called a Zero Bottle (because it was cooled to a fraction of a degree above Absolute Zero).

During the slow trip to Number Five, Emery was thoughtful and silent.

His search had actually begun. That golden light on the screen was the first star. And there were planets circling it.

The waiting, the loneliness would be over soon. He was sure of it.

If not this star, the next.

There were almost two hundred on his itinerary.

If not the next, the one after that.

Brothers.

Number Five.

Christopher's read-out: "Gas giant. Dead. Always was."

Short Elsie jump.

Laser thrust for six days.

Number Four.

"Gas giant. Dead. Always was."

Short Elsie jump.

Laser thrust for five days.

Number Three.

"Volcanic. Mostly methane atmosphere. D-e-a-d."

So were Numbers Two and One.

"Bad result," Emery said, "but a good start. The process works. The equipment works."

"You mean *me*?"

"I mean everything. *Including* you."

"Thanks, boss."

Emery said, "I'm even beginning to get used to Elsie."

"So am I."

"You? You can't get used to things. You don't *feel* anything, do you?"

"Of course I do."

There was that smug tone again. How could an android be smug?

Emery said, "That's not possible."

"You mean I'm having delusions?"

"That's not possible, either."

"Emery, trust me: I can feel every emotion you can feel."

"But you're a machine."

"So are you. The difference is, your parts grow naturally. Mine have to be manufactured."

Emery wondered if Christopher was beginning to malfunction.

He looked exactly like a very small, very serious young man, with thick, brown hair (that never needed trimming), intelligent brown eyes (that never needed sleep), a compact, sturdy body (that never needed food), dressed in a miniature, tan Explorer's jumpsuit.

Emery said, "Machines don't have feelings."

"Until now, they didn't. But I was designed to be a Companion—to live and work with a human being for years—in the cramped environment of a ship—and in dangerous places we've never been before. Would you like to spend all that time with a cold, emotionless robot? No way, Jose. So they gave me emotions—the same ones you've got. Haven't you noticed?"

"Unfortunately, I have."

"Why 'unfortunately'?"

"I just want to concentrate on what we're doing. On the search. That's what I'm here for. I don't need a friend."

"I'm *not* a friend; I'm a Companion. And I'm a breakthrough. The first android with a heart—figuratively speaking, of course. The only one of its kind."

"Do me a favor. Keep it to yourself."

"Whatever you say, boss."

The next star was planetless. As was the star after that one.

Then they jumped to Capella, which had one planet orbiting it—a gas giant fifteen times the size of Jupiter, too large to be a genuine planet, too small to ignite the nuclear fires that would make it a star.

Emery said, "A sad fate. Imagine spending billions of years wishing you'd become a sun, knowing you'd never be one. And all the time, Capella is showing off with its light and heat, right there in your neighhorhood."

"Hey, it's nice to hear your voice again. Does this mean that you're finally coming out of your shell?"

"I told you that I don't talk much."

"Emery, we're going to be out here for years. Just you and me and the Universe. A little conversation wouldn't kill you."

"What should we talk about?"

"The ship. The search. Any old thing at all."

"Christopher, I've never even shared my thoughts with *people*. Why would I want to share them with a—with you?"

The little android smiled. "Did I just detect a trace of sympathy? You were going to say, 'with a machine,' but you spared my feelings. That's a giant leap for mankind, *n'est-ce pas*?"

Emery, caught in the act, couldn't help smiling.

Christopher repeated, "My feelings."

"Your feelings."

"So now you believe I *have* feelings."

"I guess I do."

"So we can start talking to each other, right?"

"Okay. But shouldn't we prepare the next Elsie jump?"

"What do you mean 'we'? Since when do *you* do any of the grunt work around here?"

Emery took the challenge.

"Fine. Why don't you just sit back and relax? I'll take care of everything."

"On second thought, I'm not so sure I want to put my life in your hands."

"You have no choice. I outrank you."

It took Emery more than thirty minutes to do what Christopher could do almost instantly. But Elsie kicked in perfectly, they disintegrated and reintegrated, and the ship was just over two billion miles from a yellow, main sequence star called Theseus B.

Christopher nodded appreciatively and said, "Well, you're not the fastest worker I've ever seen, but that was a good jump."

"I'll scan for planets, too."

"Will wonders never cease?"

Emery began the read-out. "Three planets. The outer one is frozen volcanic rock. Dead."

"Don't get discouraged. We've only just begun."

Emery handled the low-powered Elsie jump with relative ease. Then he switched to the laser thrust engine.

He sat back, sighed and said, "Nothing to it."

He asked the dispenser for a cup of coffee, which it delivered almost immediately.

He took a long sip. "Okay, Christopher, let's talk."

The android smiled and settled himself on his favorite perch—a steel shelf opposite Emery's chair.

"So tell me about your hopes and dreams."

"I'd rather not. Why don't you tell me who programmed your vocabulary. Your choice of words is a little—strange."

Christopher sighed and said, "It's difficult for me to talk about all that pre-natal stuff: how I was built, how my circuits were installed, how I was programmed. I know it happened, and I was aware of some of it, but it seems so remote. It's like asking you what it was like to be a fetus."

"Never mind. I don't want to make you uncomfortable."

"I can tell you this: the person who programmed my vocabulary—my style—even my voice—made me a mirror image of himself. His name is Featherstone. He's supposed to be a genius. But he's also a flake."

Emery laughed. "Which makes you a *son* of a flake."

"I guess so. But at least he was always honest with me. Some of the other people who worked on me treated me like a *thing*. They gave me feelings, but they didn't respect those feelings. Featherstone respected me.

And he told me something that no one else did. He told me that they would never build another Companion like me."

"What do you mean?"

"They would never build another android with feelings. Machines had no right to feel anything. So I'm the beginning and the end of my species. Featherstone told me that."

"And they gave you to *me*. What a gift!"

"Now let's talk about you."

Emery sipped his coffee thoughtfully for a minute, then asked, "What would you like to know?"

"Were you always the strong, silent type?"

Emery smiled and nodded.

He said, "I grew up in a very quiet home."

"Did you ever have any fun?"

"Not really."

"You poor bastard."

"What the hell do you know about fun?"

"Whatever Featherstone told me. And he thought that if you didn't enjoy something, you shouldn't do it."

"He's right. But there are different ways to enjoy things. It's not always about 'fun.'"

"So what else is it about?"

"Satisfaction."

"Why do you care so much about the Search?"

"I don't want to believe that in a universe with trillions of stars—trillions of possibilities—human beings are all alone, stuck in an unimportant corner of an ordinary galaxy, circling an average star. I don't want to believe that there's no one else out here. That scares me. It's like living in one small room in a huge house—and knowing that no one has ever lived in any of the other rooms, and no one ever will."

"And that matters to you?"

"It always has."

"And you call *me* a flake?"

Emery finished his coffee.

He said, "I'm tired, Christopher. Lights out in a few minutes. We've talked enough."

"For now," Christopher said. "For now."

The simulated days and nights came and went. Emery and Christopher searched—from star to star—from planet to planet—and found nothing but stars and planets.

Sometimes Emery was silent. Sometimes he was willing to talk to Christopher.

Once, six months into the voyage, they both took a Walk on the Wild Side.

They stood together on a sliver of metal in the star-spattered blackness, almost a billion miles from a golden-yellow sun, millions of miles from a barren, frozen planet.

They couldn't speak to each other, but they could communicate: Christopher could send—and receive—telepathic messages.

At first, to Emery, telepathy was almost as unpleasant as Elsie. It was like eavesdropping on someone else's mind.

Then, after a while, the process became more comfortable and Emery could separate his "voice" from Christopher's. And they could talk to each other. It just took a little practice.

Emery thought, "You're not cold out here?"

"My instruments register the temperature, but I don't feel heat and cold."

"And you don't need air or food. You could survive just about anywhere."

"If you've got it, flaunt it."

"Incredible view, huh?"

"Yes."

"Makes you feel so small."

"I *am* small. Or hadn't you noticed?"

"Here you are, facing eternity, and you can't be serious."

"I'm too small to be serious."

"Two more planets in this system."

"Two more chances."

Emery reached out his hand, which was enclosed by the glove of his pressure suit. He pretended to hold the distant golden-yellow star on his fingertips. He could almost feel the warmth of it, a billion miles away.

And, at the same time, he could almost feel the coldness of the empty space between them.

How empty is it? Emery thought.

Christopher didn't answer him.

More than one Earth year had passed. Their search was moving quickly—too quickly. Most of the stars they visited were planetless. And when there *were* planets, they were dead. One long Elsie jump, a quick survey, and they moved on.

The conversations between Emery and Christopher were sometimes spoken, and sometimes telepathic. Emery became quite adept at telepathy and even preferred it when he was tired. He could close his eyes and rest, and still keep up his side of the conversation.

But he was beginning to lose hope. They had already explored half of the stars on their itinerary and they had found nothing.

The process had become a blur of disappointment. Emery gave Christopher more and more of the responsibility for handling the ship and the sensors.

Then they jumped to a star called Medusa. It had a family of four planets.

The inner two were too close to Medusa to sustain life: too much heat, too much radiation.

The planet furthest out was frozen gas—a methane popsicle, Christopher called it.

As they approached the third planet, Emery watched its image on the video-screen absently, without much interest.

It was about the size of Earth. Its atmosphere was very thin and transparent: no oxygen, no water, just a scattering of inert gases. The surface was incredibly smooth and uniform, a Venus-like expanse of ancient, hardened lava, unmarked by rivers or canyons or meteoric craters or seismic disturbances—devoid of surface features.

Except for one dark brown ripple on the ocher face of the planet—a ridge about 300 feet high, a mile long and half a mile wide. Four deep gouges ran up one side of the ridge, like a huge flight of steps, and the top of it was a broad mesa.

Apparently, like its namesake, Medusa had turned the third planet to stone.

Christopher began to scan it.

He smiled and said, "Pay dirt!"

Emery's stomach tightened. He leaned toward Christopher.

He said, very softly, "Tell me. Tell me."

"There's life on that planet. Organic, growing, changing, repairing itself. And *thinking*!"

"Thinking? How do you know that?"

"Not from the ship's sensors, Emery. I can *feel* the thoughts. I'll show you."

Christopher opened a telepathic gate and pushed a stream of alien images into Emery's mind: flaming, underground rivers of heat and light, felt rather than seen; dark, massive, subsurface towers of frozen lava; lightless, sinuous tunnels, snaking through buried mountain ranges.

No words, no thoughts. Just an incoherent, grammarless language of the senses.

Emery closed the telepathic gate. The images were too chaotic for him to handle.

He said, "Why are their minds so confused? Why is it such a jumble?"

"I don't know. We'll find out."

"Where are they? Not on the surface. Below it?"

"On the surface and below it."

Emery watched the screen as the ship's video camera moved closer and closer to the planet. The image was unchanging: smooth, hard, featureless.

"There's nothing on the surface."

"*One* thing. That ridge."

"Is that where they are? Inside the ridge? Below it?"

Christopher ignored the ship's instrument panel. He was reaching out with his own telepathic sensor. He didn't answer Emery for several minutes, as DeepSpEx XII descended toward the planet.

Then he said, "One mind. One voice."

"You can only sense one mind?"

"There is only one living being on the planet."

"Somewhere in that ridge? The survivor of a disaster? The last of his race?"

Christopher shook his head.

He said, "There never *was* another. There never *will* be."

"How do you know that?"

"I've contacted it. It doesn't have words. It senses that I exist but it doesn't understand what I am—or *how* I can exist. When we land, we'll learn all about each other."

"But where is it? In the ridge? Below the ridge?"

"Neither and both: it *is* the ridge."

The ship landed a few hundred feet from the ridge, searing a black circle in the yellow lava rock. Emery opened the hatch and climbed down the narrow ladder. Christopher, in his tan jump suit, was right behind him.

Emery walked without effort in the almost-Earth gravity. His pressure suit was slim and flexible. His tinted, transparent helmet fed him breathable air and gave him an unobstructed view of the smooth, barren surface, the ridge, the black sky, the distant stars and yellow Medusa, hanging like an ominous lantern above the horizon.

He thought, This place is a nightmare. There's life here?

Christopher answered, Intelligent life. An *enormous* intelligence, *enormous* capacity. It never had a need for words. It never had to communicate. It fed on images, sensations, and its own imaginings. And now it's learning what language is—what words are—from me—so quickly that, by the time we reach the ridge, it will be able to speak to us.

They walked across the empty plain, Medusa behind them, looking over their shoulders, casting their long, pale shadows on the ground.

The ridge, which had seemed so tiny on the video screen, loomed like a mountain ahead of them.

Then, in their minds, they heard a new voice—a tentative voice—that seemed to be testing every word it thought.

The new voice said, "I didn't know there were others."

Christopher expanded the statement: "Other *beings*."

"I didn't know there were other beings."

Emery: "There are no other beings here?"

"There never have been. I am here now. I was here always. I will be here always."

They had almost reached the ridge. It was not hardened lava. It was dark and porous, and it shimmered in Medusa's yellow light. Long, shallow ripples moved slowly, continuously, over its surface, like waves in a sea of molasses.

Emery asked Christopher, "What material is that?"

Christopher didn't know.

The new voice said, "Silicon-carbon rings, crystals of matter, elements pulled from the rocks, the lava rivers. Self-repairing, self-replicating. Dispersed intelligence: everywhere, nowhere in particular."

Emery said, "Self-replicating? But aren't you the only living thing here?"

The new voice said, "I add to myself. I grow myself. I am many. I am one."

Christopher's telepathic voice spoke slowly, as if he were translating an image: "A colony with millions of bodies that become one body. Millions of minds that think as one mind."

Emery and the little android stood silently on the smooth lava plain, a few feet from the shimmering ridge. Questions and answers—words and images—raced back and forth. Human thoughts—computer thoughts—alien thoughts—flooded the silence.

Christopher said, "Tell us about yourself," and it did.

It said that it was immobile. But its mind could travel.

It plunged into the molten core of its planet, and traced the glowing streams of magma that flowed through subterranean canyons.

It soared into space, to the other planets in the system. And sometimes it touched the fiery face of Medusa and burrowed into the nuclear fires of the star's interior.

For its own pleasure, it fashioned worlds of imagination, conjuring up fantastic dream landscapes more beautiful than any it had seen.

It played with colors and shapes, with light and darkness, like an abstract painter.

It knew that there were other stars, other galaxies, too far for its mind to reach.

It believed that there were no boundaries, no limits, no barriers to its dreaming.

But it had never imagined another living being. It had never thought that it was alone, because there never seemed to be an alternative.

Now there was.

Emery and Christopher told it about a world where billions of individual creatures lived—from one-celled plants and animals through the whole evolutionary chain—to people, families, cities, nations.

They told it about birth and death.

They told it about romance and science and politics.

They told it about space travel and the Search.

Medusa had set. Emery was exhausted.

He said, "I need some sleep."

It never slept, never rested. They told it about sleep.

Christopher wasn't tired, of course. He asked Emery if he could stay and continue the conversation.

"Sure. Take notes."

When Emery returned to the ship, he tried to understand why he didn't feel excited, or satisfied, or relieved.

The Search is over, he thought. *I've found what I was looking for.*

But he felt cold and empty.

He was almost too tired to fall asleep. And when he finally did, he dreamed of places that no man had ever seen.

When he awoke, hours later, he didn't feel refreshed. He washed, brushed his teeth.

He checked the video screen. Medusa had risen over the ridge. Christopher was still standing in the same place.

Emery asked the dispenser for scrambled eggs, a toasted English muffin and coffee. He ate his breakfast quickly. Then he went back to the ridge.

As he approached, he could tune in on their conversation. They were exchanging ideas so quickly that the words and images overlapped. He couldn't make sense of them.

It was almost as if *Emery* had become the alien.

He interrupted the flow with his own thoughts.

"Christopher, have you recorded all the information we need?"

"Yes."

"Then it's time to go back."

"Right."

The little android didn't move.

"Christopher, let's go."

The android turned to look at Emery. Its dark brown eyes seemed remote and lifeless.

The other voice—the alien voice—said, "Don't go. I didn't know that I was alone. If you go, I will be lonely."

Emery said, "We must return and bring back the news that we've found you. We must go."

The voice said, "*You* can go, Emery. But Christopher must stay. He is my brother."

"Christopher?"

The android smiled at Emery. It was a calm, peaceful smile.

Christopher said, "We *are* the same. We are not born. We do not die. Our minds can grow and expand and learn forever. We are self-repairing, indestructible. We can teach each other. We can become each other. And each of us is unique—alone—one of a kind. The first of our race, and the last. If I stay here, I won't be alone. *Neither* of us will be."

Emery didn't know how to respond.

Christopher said, "I know what you're searching for. But you've been looking in the wrong places. You *aren't* unique. You *aren't* alone."

Emery watched the slow waves shimmer on the face of the ridge.

Then he said, "I'll tell them that you self-destructed. That your emotions got the better of you."

"They'll believe that, because they want to."

"And I won't tell anyone what we found here. This will be just another dead star system. No one will ever come back."

"Thank you, Emery."

"Goodbye, Christopher."

"Goodbye."

When he reached the ship, Emery turned back to look at them. Christopher had climbed onto the ridge and was sitting there, a tiny figure outlined by Medusa's yellow glow.

Brothers.

Emery knew that he still had a hundred stars to explore. But that thought no longer excited him.

Because, for the first time in his life, Emery Harmon wanted to go home.

II

OTHER CHOICES

THE BUSKER

It was the coldest New England winter in years. In Fairfield, Connecticut, there was very little snow but, day after day, a steady, bitter northeastern wind kept the temperature close to zero.

David Hutchins didn't mind the weather. He hardly noticed it, even on the eight-block walk, morning and night, to and from the railroad station. Waiting for the express to New York City, he bought a cup of coffee at the Dunkin' Donuts stand on the platform and drank it in the waiting room, rushing outside to board the train at the last minute. His office was only a ten-minute walk from Grand Central Station.

David's fortieth birthday was in November. Except for an occasional sinus headache, he was healthy.

He worked in the marketing department of a telecommunications company as the vice president's right hand man. He organized departmental meetings, wrote speeches and presentations for his boss, developed the semi-annual marketing plan, and edited a monthly marketing newsletter.

The vice president was an abusive man, but David ignored his abuse, just as he ignored the cold weather: neither was preventable.

David was well paid. He often worked late and sometimes worked on the weekend, but that didn't matter any more.

Late on one bitterly cold night, a few days before Christmas, David was walking home from the station. The streets were almost deserted. When he crossed Post Road, the icy wind attacked him, but there was a puzzling undertone to its angry roar: the sound of a violin.

As he walked up the block, the music grew louder and he saw the violinist at the next corner. She was a tall, slender woman in her early twenties, dressed in dark slacks, a dark, heavy coat and a black fur hat that covered her hair and her ears. An open violin case lay at her feet. There were a few donations in it: the coins held a couple of bills in place, preventing them from flying away in the wind.

She was playing a sweet, mournful tune, her chin resting on the glossy wooden body of the instrument, her dark brown eyes focused on some distant place he couldn't see.

David watched the long, graceful fingers of her left hand dance up and down the neck of the violin, pressing the strings against invisible frets. Her right hand moved the bow in rhythmic thrusts, a visual echo of the music's flow.

He wondered why she was still out here in the street so late, when there was little chance that anyone would pass by. And her bare hands must be frozen!

He stopped a few feet from her.

Music, popular or classical, had never been important to David. His wife had liked jazz, which he didn't enjoy. His daughter had listened to the kind of music the violinist was playing.

A vigorous downstroke of the bow ended the piece. The violinist looked at David for the first time. He realized that he was staring at her.

He asked, "Aren't you cold out here?"

She smiled and said softly, almost too softly to hear over the wind, "I'm fine."

Her smile reminded him of someone.

He said, "It's late. Why don't you go home? There's no one in the street."

"You're here."

He took off his glove, reached into his pocket and found a couple of bills. He selected a five-dollar bill and held it out for her. She took it from him. Her fingers were warm.

"Thank you."

"You should go home now."

"I'm fine."

He shrugged and started to walk past her. She began to play again. This time, he recognized the melody: he had heard it many times. It was on one of his daughter's CDs.

He stopped, turned toward her and listened. This time, she watched him as she played. Looking into her eyes, he could almost anticipate the next musical phrase. The notes climbed and swooped down and rushed forward in a beautiful frenzy. And then it was over.

He said, "Who wrote that?"

"Bach. You've heard it before?"

"Yes. I think so."

She smiled again. He wondered what color her hair was.

He said, "Please, do me a favor: let me buy you some coffee or tea and something to eat."

"Aren't *you* doing *me* a favor?"

"I hope so."

She moved the bow to her left hand, bent over and scooped up the money in the violin case, putting it in her coat pocket, and then put the instrument and bow in the case, locking it.

There was a coffee shop open on Post Road. Except for the woman behind the counter, no one else was there.

The violinist ordered black coffee and a blueberry muffin. David ordered just coffee.

When they sat down, she put the violin case on a chair, pulled off the fur hat and dropped it onto the case.

Her hair was deep brown, thick and straight, and cut short.

David said, "It's a shame you have to do this."

"I love my music."

"No, I mean—that you have to—be out on the street like that."

She took a bite of the muffin and a sip of coffee before she said, "I'm doing what I want to do."

He extended his hand.

"My name is David."

She took his hand but hesitated for a moment.

He thought, *It's as if she needs time to invent a name for herself.*

Then she said, "I'm Diane."

"Do you live in Fairfield, Diane?"

"Sometimes."

She smiled at him and, again, there was something familiar in the smile, but he couldn't identify it.

He said, "I hope you *do* have a place to go tonight. You do, don't you?"

"Why are you so worried about me? Do I look sick? Do I look frightened? Do I look like someone you should be worried about?"

"No."

She nibbled on the muffin, drank some more coffee and asked, "Do *you* have a place to go?"

"Of course."

"Then what are you doing out in the street so late, on a cold, cold night like this?"

She laughed. David had to smile.

He said, "I worked late. I was on my way home."

"Then that's where you should be. You'll be missed."

"No, that's not a problem."

He looked into her eyes again and, again, he could almost hear her music.

He asked, "Have you played professionally anywhere?"

"You mean, 'anywhere *else*.'"

He nodded.

She said, "Yes. But I prefer to be a busker."

"A busker?"

"That's what the British call it."

"You mean, a 'beggar.'"

Her response was patient and pedagogical: "I mean, a 'street musician'—a 'strolling entertainer.' A busker, not a beggar. I play my music, and people reward me for it."

To David, that seemed like an evasion, rather than an explanation, but he said, "I understand."

She finished the muffin and took a last sip of coffee.

She said, "David, it's time for you to go home."

"Is it? It's just a house. In the Spring, I'm going to put it on the market."

Diane arose, put on her fur hat and picked up her violin case. She extended her hand. David stood up, too, and shook her hand.

She said, "Thank you."

She turned and began to leave the coffee shop without waiting for him to join her.

Then she stopped for a moment, turned to him and said, "Don't worry about me," and left the coffee shop.

He sat down again and finished his coffee slowly. When he left the shop and walked home, she was nowhere in sight.

The next day at the office, Alice Kramer, David's assistant, was in a somber mood. He didn't ask her for an explanation. But she unburdened herself anyway, as she always did.

She said, "Brian left me. When I got home last night, he was gone. Gone with the wind. All of his clothes, his books, the rest of his shit. He didn't even leave a note."

Alice was a small, thin, humorless woman in her mid-thirties. She had worked for David for almost five years, during which time her apartment had been a temporary rest stop for a seemingly endless train of men—a blur of feckless parasites whose comings and goings left her sadder, but no wiser.

Instead of saying, "What did you expect? What do you ever expect?" David rewarded her with an understanding, sympathetic nod. But he resented the constant intrusion of her absurdly melancholy life: it forced him to go back, to remember, and to resurrect his anger.

She said, "I thought it would be different this time," but she sounded unconvinced and unconvincing.

They were sitting in a conference room, at one end of a long table. David looked past Alice, through the window behind her, at a corner of Central Park. Bare, gray trees shuddered in a harsh, icy, cross-town wind. The sky was smeared with dark clouds—a mirror-image of the dirt-streaked, slush-covered streets.

He remembered Julia on smiling summer evenings at Shakespeare-in-the-Park: the hot starlight reflected in her cool, gray eyes; the soft ripple of her laugh at something he said; the long, graceful flow of her walk. She was the serene eye of the hurricane, quiet and calm and lovely, a sanctuary in the midst of the storm. She held his hand and kissed his mouth and he let the rest of the world rush by.

Alice was still talking about Brian. She couldn't understand why he had left her. She really couldn't.

David could.

Then he thought of his own empty house, and Alice seemed much less foolish.

That night at eleven-thirty, on his walk home from the station, the busker wasn't there.

He thought, *I'll probably never see her again*.

He was wrong. The next night, a Friday night, he took an earlier train. It was only a few minutes after ten when he arrived in Fairfield.

She wasn't on the same corner, however. She was on a less traveled street, further from the center of town, much closer to his house. She was wearing the same dark outfit, the same coat and hat, but there was no money in her open violin case.

The northeast wind was a razor of ice. Dense clouds obscured the moon and the stars. But as he approached her, the supple voice of her violin was like the glowing logs in a fireplace, radiating warmth and comfort.

He stood and listened and watched her shape the music with her hands and her eyes. A soaring ladder of notes spiraled up from the bow and punctured the darkness with a shaft of invisible light.

He was certain that this was another piece of music that was one of his daughter's favorites.

She finished with a fierce downstroke on two strings. The final chord hovered between them for a moment before it disappeared.

David said, "Diane, I'm . . ."

He wanted to say, "I'm glad to see you," but he didn't.

She smiled and said, "Working late again, huh?"

He nodded.

He said, "This is a terrible location. You should be out on Post Road. Nobody ever walks by here."

"*You* did."

He thought, *It's as if she knows where I live*.

He said, "We're only a couple of blocks from my house. Would you like some soup—some coffee—something to eat?"

"You should have been a social worker."

"You're not going to make any money here anyway."

She smiled.

He said, "And I'm not hitting on you. So you don't have to worry about that."

She said, very seriously, "I'm not worried."

Then she packed her violin and bow in the case and asked, "Do you have any cookies?"

"Chocolate chip."

"Perfect. Say no more," she said, and put her arm through his. "Lead the way."

When she touched him, he was almost disappointed: she had become real.

Of course she's real, he thought. *Of course she is.*

Diane was very quiet as she sat in the kitchen.

When David was pouring her second cup of coffee, she said, "This is a beautiful house. Why do you want to sell it?"

"I don't need a house. It's too big for one person. I'm thinking of getting an apartment in the city—New York City. Then I'd be closer to work."

"Your work is important to you?"

David smiled.

"No. It would just be easier to get there every day."

"If you don't care about your work, why do you stay late all the time?"

"It's the nature of the job. And I would just as soon be at the office as be here."

She nodded.

He said, "When my wife and daughter were here, it was different."

She nodded again.

He said, "When you finish, would you play something for me?" He smiled. "I assume you can play *indoors*, too?"

"If I have to."

She played for him in the family room—up a short flight of steps from the foyer. It was a high-ceilinged, cluttered, lived-in room with a brick fireplace at one end. David had started a fire when they arrived at the house. Now it was crackling cozily, brightly.

He sat on a leather couch near the fireplace. She stood in the center of the room and played, her image flickering in the light of the burning logs, the sound filling the room from wall to wall like a featherbed of music.

He watched the dark, fluid shadow of her body dance to its own melody, turning, thrusting, melting the boundary between the violin and the hands that played it, until the shadow and the sound were one.

Afterward, he could never recall how long she played, or how many pieces. And when she stopped, he could still hear the music.

She said, "I've got to go now."

"You can sleep here tonight, if you want to. There are plenty of extra rooms."

"Thank you. But I can't."

When she was gone, he went back to the family room and watched the fire in the fireplace and heard her music. He heard it all weekend.

That Saturday afternoon, David's younger brother Martin called. Martin worked for Texas Instruments, designing chips and integrated circuits. He lived in Richardson, Texas. He was married to a lawyer. They had agreed not to have any children: they were too busy for children.

"Davey, it's your smarter brother. How are you?"

"Fine. How are you doing?"

"Great. Great."

"How's Michele?"

"Feeling pretty sassy. She just won a major case: software piracy, or something. I'm not sure of the details, but she made a bundle."

"Well, at least you won't be hitting me up for a loan."

Martin laughed. Then he got to the point.

"We'd love to see you, Davey. We'd love for you to visit us for a couple of weeks."

"Thanks, Marty, but not right now."

"Jesus, you must be freezing your ass off! I've been reading about how cold it is up in Connecticut. Why not take a break?"

"I'm too busy."

"Davey, it's not good for you to be alone so much."

"What makes you think I'm alone? I'm not alone. How can you be alone in New York City? I'm fine."

"Are you seeing anyone?"

"You mean dating?"

"Yes, I mean dating."

"No."

"Why not?"

"I think I've done enough damage."

"You didn't do anything. Julia did."

"Marty, I'm not in the mood to talk about it."

"But you act as if it was your fault. It wasn't."

"I didn't make her happy. So she left me. That's the whole story."

"And Kathie—that wasn't your fault, either."

David hesitated before he answered: "No, it wasn't," but the words were cold and thick.

"Davey, please come down here. I'm sure you've got plenty of vacation time you haven't used."

"Maybe in a few months. Not now. I've got a lot to do at work. Big conference coming up."

Marty gave up.

He said, "Well, take care of yourself. And remember, it's an open offer. We love you."

"Thanks, Marty. I'll talk to you soon."

Marty laughed. "Only if *I* call *you*."

A few days later, on a frozen, windless Tuesday night, the busker was there again. She was wearing a different outfit, a long, dark brown coat, a brown fur hat, an ankle-length, dark brown skirt and leather boots. She was playing sweeter, less angular music. For some reason, David thought that it sounded like nineteenth century Viennese music; waltzy, spirited, beer and schnitzel music.

She smiled at him and he returned the smile. He listened for a time and, when she had completed her third piece, he said, "Diane, I have a suggestion."

"Get out of the business?"

"No, no: the money is too good."

She laughed, and the sound echoed softly through the empty streets.

He said, "I'll bet you've worked up quite an appetite out here. And I skipped dinner tonight: I just never got to it. So let's pick up my car and go to the diner in Southport—just a few minutes from here. And we can have something to eat. Breakfast, lunch, dinner—you name it."

"Are you trying to fatten me up for the kill?"

"I just enjoy talking to you."

"But you don't know me. Or is it *because* you don't know me."

He shrugged.

She said, "Okay. Let's go."

Twenty minutes later, she was taking healthy bites out of a cheeseburger, and he was eating a tuna melt.

She ate quickly, in a no-nonsense, matter-of-fact way. She picked up her french fries with her long, graceful fingers and dipped them in a glob of ketchup before she devoured them.

When she had made a sizeable dent in her meal, he said, "I'd like to tell you about some things. Do you mind?"

"That depends on what you're going to tell me. And by the time you finish, it'll be too late to mind, won't it?"

He nodded.

She said, "Go ahead."

He said, "A little more than a year ago, my wife Julia left me."

"And you still love her."

"It's more than that. My whole life was about pleasing her, about being with her, satisfying her, giving her what she wanted. I've never loved any woman but her. I could sit and look at her for hours, listen to her voice, her laugh, watch her move. I was addicted to her."

"How long were you married?"

"Fifteen years. And one night, when I came home from work, she told me that she was leaving me. She said that she had been seeing another man for more than a year. She loved him the way she had never loved me. He was exciting, dangerous—that's the word she used: dangerous. I couldn't give her what he gave her. And she didn't want to waste the rest of her life with me.

"I was suddenly no one. For her, all the beautiful days and nights that meant so much to me, meant nothing. I didn't know what to say. My hands were shaking. My throat was tight and dry.

"I asked her, 'What about Kathie?' Our daughter.

"She said, 'I can't take care of her. My plans—our plans—are too flexible. We're going to be traveling a lot. She's not that strong. She's better off with you. You love her more than I do, anyway. I've never been the maternal type.' A few days later, she was gone."

The busker sipped her coffee and waited for him to go on.

"Kathie—she was twelve at the time—wasn't as surprised as I was. She knew her mother better than I did. But that didn't make it easier for her."

"Have you heard from your wife?"

"No. She disappeared. She didn't even divorce me. She just went her own way."

He didn't say anything more. Diane finished her cheeseburger and fries.

"Is this the first time you've talked about what happened?"

"Yes."

"Do you feel a little better?"

"A little."

She said, "Good."

She began to gather her coat, her hat and her violin case.

"Thank you for dinner. I've got to be going."

"Let me drive you home."

"No. That's not necessary."

"I wish . . ."

"Don't wish, David. Wishes usually don't come true."

She left. He ordered another cup of coffee, and thought about the end of his story. That would be much more difficult to tell her. But he knew that he would.

And then, on the drive home, and for the rest of the night, he started to think more about Diane. Where did she live? Why was she always there when he came home? Or *almost* always.

It seemed to him that her music, her smile, her gestures were familiar, but he couldn't place them.

And sometimes he had the feeling that she already knew what he was going to say.

He fell asleep thinking about her.

David didn't see her again for a week. He was very late getting home, but the weather had finally improved. It was a clear, starlit, brisk night. He heard her music from several blocks away—thick, proud chords and a fiery melody line that reached up toward the full moon.

She was two blocks from his house.

He dropped a ten dollar bill into her violin case and stood watching her. She was in black again and this time, as she played, she looked into his eyes. He couldn't read her expression.

When she had finished the piece she was playing, she took the money she had collected out of the case and put it into her pocket, returned her violin and bow to the case and said, "Where to?"

"My house, if you don't mind. Coffee and chocolate chip cookies."

She took his arm and said, "Let's go," but her voice sounded strained and mechanical, as if she would rather not go with him.

They sat across from each other at the kitchen table. She chewed absently on a cookie and waited.

David wasn't sure how to begin.

He said, "When Julia left me, at first I was disoriented. I hadn't planned a life without her. She was always at the center of things. And our daughter, Kathie, was too much like a reminder of Julia. She looked like her, although she was gentler, quieter. She loved music—the kind of music you play—and she wasn't very strong. Physically, I mean. She couldn't go to gym. She got tired very easily. It was her heart. It hadn't developed the way it should have. The chances are, she would need surgery in a couple of years."

He stopped, searched the woodgrain of the kitchen table for a moment, then continued.

"At first, I was lost without Julia. Then I became angry. I was angry all the time. I didn't want to be home. I didn't want to see Kathie's face. It was like seeing Julia's ghost—but a ghost that was much more loving than she could ever be. That made me even angrier. I began to work late a lot. We have a neighbor—a very nice older lady—a widow—who kept an eye on Kathie for me."

He wrapped his fingers around his coffee cup. "It was as if I was blaming Kathie for what her mother had done to me. Julia had hurt me. But she had hurt Kathie, too. My daughter was a very fragile person. I loved her very much, but my anger kept us apart. She couldn't fight it."

He put down his coffee cup, stood up and walked around the table to the window. He looked out at the shadows of the trees against the cold, star-flecked night sky.

"I kept telling myself that I would make it up to her—soon. That the anger would recede—soon. That I would love Kathie so much—that I would tell her how much I loved her—and she would be fine—we would be fine together. But I was angry at her, too, because I knew that she wasn't healthy—that she could die—that she could leave me, too."

David turned to look at Diane.

"One morning, I got a call at the office. Kathie was sitting at her desk in school and she leaned forward, as if she was tired, and she seemed to have fallen asleep. But she was dead. And what had I given her? Anger. Nothing else. I had never said, 'I love you, sweetheart, and you'll always have me to depend on.' I gave her nothing. And she died far away from me, far away from my love."

His eyes were filled with tears, but he spoke so clearly that, if you didn't look at him, you wouldn't know that he was crying.

"And I'll never be able to change that. I don't believe in God and Heaven and all that crap. I never pray to anyone. When you die, you die. She's gone, and I'll never be able to tell her how much I love her."

Diane stood up and went over to David.

She put her hands on his shoulders and said, "Kathie loved you more than anyone else. And she knew how much you loved her."

"I didn't tell her."

"She knows. I'm sure that she knows," she said, and she smiled.

David studied Diane's face, her eyes, her expression, her smile.

He nodded his head.

He said, "I understand. Now I understand. That's who you are. I should have recognized you."

She repeated, "She knows."

She turned away from him. Her coat and hat were on a kitchen chair. She put them on, and picked up her violin case.

She left the room, looking back at him when she reached the door, and smiled.

He didn't move.

It was very clear to him now.

He thought, "Maybe I won't sell the house in the Spring. Maybe I'll stay here. I don't have to go."

He didn't sell the house. He stayed.

David Hutchins had never believed in God. And he had never prayed. But finally he had something to pray for.

He prayed that he would never see Diane again.

WEEKEND

Roger Schubert's life was altogether fitting and proper for a magazine editor with his talent ("I can usually make a so-so story good, and a good story, great"), his convictions ("I doubt if there is a God, but people should be kind to each other anyway, I guess"), his life experience ("I'm old-fashioned: I believe in love, marriage and children—in that order!"), and his age ("I'll be fifty-seven next month, but I don't feel a day over fifty-five").

He was *content*. ("Happiness is for idiots," he observed.) He and his wife Irene still loved each other and were the best of friends. There were times when he would have preferred a more seductive mate ("but nobody's perfect"). And, after all, as he admitted (but only to himself), his own sensuality was, perhaps, more theoretical than factual.

But he was past all that by now, wasn't he? He enjoyed his work at *Weekend* magazine and was well (though not extravagantly) paid for it. He and Irene lived in a comfortable home in Fairfield, Connecticut. They had two successful sons, each of whom was married to a nice-enough woman, each of whom had two children, and each of whom lived in Westport, the town next door, and about a half-step higher on the prestige scale.

In short, in this chaotic, dreary world in which so many innocents are caught in the crossfire of history, Roger Schubert, who had his health, a steady job he enjoyed, and a nice family, really had nothing to complain about.

Until he met Elizabeth Schaefer, *Weekend's* new Director of Information Services.

In the beginning, five or six years ago, when the Powers That Be had established her department, he had protested: "*Information Services!* It isn't enough to publish a classy, well-written, beautifully designed magazine any more: now we have to put everything *on-line*. Click, click, click. Instead of leading the *rats* out of town, The Pied Piper is leading the *mouses* into it!"

Weekend was a detailed, sophisticated guide to the multitudinous pleasures of the Tri-State Area, from fine eateries and luxurious hotels to Classical, Jazz and Rock Concerts, The Theater (Broadway, Off-Broadway, Off-Off-Broadway), the Opera, the Dance and the Cinema. And, in fact, the Internet was the perfect way for the (stereo)typical, frantic, fast moving, trendy, high income, Nanny-assisted, Tri-State couple (and their unmarried compatriots), to tune into the latest scoop on What's Hot and What's Not.

So *Weekend* magazine became a mere appendage of its dot.com website.

I can see that my future is behind me, Roger said to himself.

When Elizabeth Schaefer joined the staff, she added a disturbing subtext to that remark.

She was young—thirty-three—a product of the Information Age (so to speak), born with a Personal Computer already installed in the nursery, no doubt. She was dark-haired, dark-eyed, pale-skinned, petite, extremely intelligent, fiercely confident, aggressive (and absolutely gorgeous).

Roger was not pleased. He preferred sailing serenely, on gentle breezes. Elizabeth was a storm that shook the masts and churned up the waves.

He had, of course, encountered many women at work, young and not so young. Although some of them were attractive, he had rarely been impressed with them and never been interested in them.

Elizabeth was something else. She matched the paradigm of Woman (shaped by Who Knows What?), locked somewhere in the vault of Roger's memory. Now, suddenly, that paradigm was rediscovered and resurrected. Alas, Poor Roger!

Elizabeth was approached by young men at the office, but she summarily rejected them. Nor did she befriend any young women who worked there. She was standoffish with everyone.

Everyone except Roger.

He had been assigned as her liaison in editorial, so it was essential for him to get to know her professionally. But she seemed determined to expand their relationship.

She arrived at work early every morning, as he did. They both liked to get a head start on the day. Soon, they were having coffee together in his office (he always let her make the first move; sometimes she was hung over or just not interested), talking about business, politics, movies and anything else that came to mind—to *her* mind, that is.

He learned quickly that she was in charge of their conversations, and he didn't object. She almost never asked him about himself, his life, or his family. She was interested in *herself*, *her* family, *her* life and the men in it.

But while she talked, occasionally soliciting his opinion, it was such a pleasure just to look at her, to listen to her voice, to wonder what it would be like to stroke her dark hair, or kiss her.

He understood that she chose him for her companion because he was convenient—intelligent, patient, willing to listen (what choice did he have?) and very middle-aged, very married, very unthreatening. She didn't have to keep her guard up, which is what she seemed to do when she was with her contemporaries.

What is she like, he wondered, *with her lovers?*

Of course, he had plenty of opportunities to hear about her lovers. Apparently, Elizabeth was involved with two men who seemed (to her, perhaps, and certainly to Roger) completely interchangeable: they both worked on the Street, but he wasn't sure if they were brokers or financial analysts or bond traders. He *was* sure (because she told him so) that they were graduates of Ivy League schools, handsome, athletic, rich and getting richer. In short, since she, too, was to the manor born and an Ivy League graduate, they were from Her Crowd.

She never referred to them with tenderness. In fact, she never referred to anyone that way, except her sister Emily. When she spoke of Emily, who was a psychologist, she really seemed to care.

Otherwise, he had the sense that she was living a fast-paced, hard-driving, exhausting life, devoid of introspection, with little time to enjoy anything.

Where is she rushing? he wondered.

Her father, who apparently had inherited wealth, was a professor of European history at Columbia University. She had great respect for him, but she spoke about him as if he had been a demanding teacher, rather than a loving parent. She rarely mentioned her mother and, when she did, it was always in a noncommittal way.

Roger admired Elizabeth's taste in music and art and books: she was solidly grounded in the classics, an atypical background for people of her generation.

She had a quick mind, a quick, sarcastic wit, and a quick temper. She was rarely angry at him, presumably because he wasn't important enough to incite her anger.

He thought about her too much—enough to generate a little guilt.

But Roger Schubert was not a creature of impulse. They worked together, they had coffee together, they had lunch together now and then (he loved to watch her chew), she spoke and he listened, life went on, and another year of Roger's life disappeared quietly.

In May, Elizabeth went to the south of France with her sister for three weeks.

Just before she left, she broke up with one of her two interchangeable men. A few weeks after she came back, still glowing with the sunshine of Provence, she broke up with Number Two.

She and Roger were having their Monday morning coffee when she told him.

She said, "I should have waited one more week: the Mary Cassatt show is opening at the Metropolitan on Friday night."

"You can go alone."

"No, no, no. There's something about an art exhibit, or a concert that doesn't work for me when I'm alone. I need someone else to share it with, to discuss it with, to look at when I feel excited by it."

"What about a friend?"

She shook her head: "My sister is at a conference, and I don't really have anyone else to go with. *At the moment,*" she added, as if she were planning to initiate a love affair or a friendship within the next few days, just so she could go to the Cassatt show.

He asked, "I guess you really like Mary Cassatt's work?"

"She was independent. She never got married. She did what she wanted to do. And she never took any shit from men."

Roger smiled. "I think she did some painting, too."

Elizabeth's eyes examined him darkly for a moment, as she decided whether or not to get angry.

Then she smiled, too. "She's a wonderful painter."

The days passed quickly for Roger, as they always did—too quickly to catch his breath. A weekly magazine is a pressure cooker.

On Thursday, Roger's wife Irene reminded him that she was spending the weekend with her mother and sister (both widows) in Mom's Westchester home. They usually got together like this every couple of months. Roger told her that he would probably stay in New York on Friday night, and maybe even Saturday night: he was working on a tighter deadline for the next issue because a multi-page advertisement had to be inserted in every copy. More time for production meant less time for editorial. He wanted to get a head start. He had made a reservation at the Marriott Marquis near Times Square.

To Irene, this was a familiar story.

On Friday morning, when Roger arrived at the office, garment bag in hand, Elizabeth wasn't there. She was working at home. The PC at her apartment was linked to *Weekend's* data-bases via the Internet, so she didn't miss a beat.

At lunch-time, Roger checked into the hotel and left his bag in the room.

At six o'clock, he decided to have a couple of drinks before he went back to the Marriott for dinner. He liked the steak house there.

It was a clear, crisp evening in June, rather cool for that time of year. There was a dark, paneled bar that he always visited on these occasions, a few blocks from the office, near 48th Street. If his favorite bartender was there, he wouldn't even have to ask for a dry Manhattan. It would appear automatically.

He found a stool near the end of the bar. He was surprised when the bartender (his favorite) saw him sit down, but didn't prepare his usual drink.

"What'll it be?" he asked.

Roger said, with quiet dignity (he hoped), "A dry Manhattan, straight up."

The bartender seemed not to know him. He delivered the drink, smiled mechanically and put the tab on the bar.

The Manhattan soothed his ruffled feathers. He drank it rather quickly, more quickly than was his custom, ate the cherry and then, catching the bartender's eye, tapped the glass for a refill.

Perhaps the poor devil has amnesia, Roger thought, as the bartender presented Dry Manhattan #2.

As he sipped his drink, Roger looked to his left, at the mirror behind the bar. He studied the images reflected in it.

Something wasn't quite right. Had the alcohol affected him that quickly? (He was drinking on an empty stomach.)

He looked at the mirror again, examining its contents more carefully. What was amiss? He continued to scan the images, but couldn't pinpoint the problem.

Then he *could*. There was one reflection missing: his own.

Roger tried to stay calm. He put his hand over his eyes for a moment. Then he lowered his hand again. In the mirror, a hand moved down from someone's eyes.

His eyes? But that wasn't *him*.

He stared at the image in the mirror, moving his hand back and forth to make sure that he was looking at the right reflection.

He was. That was Roger Schubert's image in the mirror—twenty years ago.

He wasn't wearing glasses. He had thick, dark brown hair. His face was unlined.

He shivered, shook his head, closed his eyes, looked again. His young face looked back at him.

What's happening to me? This is impossible!

Roger glanced down at his suit, his tie. They were the same. He took his wallet out of his pocket. The date on his Metro North ticket was correct. The dates on his credit card and his *Weekend* ID were correct. The two free passes to the Boston Symphony concert were for tomorrow night.

The picture on his driver's license showed a young Roger, but his birth date was listed as September 8, 1941.

He was younger—and he wasn't. He didn't know what to do.

He finished his Manhattan and paid the bill. He walked out into the cool June evening.

His step was quicker.

Fifty-seven-year-old Roger was as slim as the thirty-five-year-old version, but now he felt a pleasant, unfamiliar tension in his arms, his chest, his legs.

How did this happen? And what if he *stayed* this way?

He went to his hotel room.

In the glare of the bathroom light, he studied his reflection in the mirror.

He touched his face, admired the taut line of his neck (no hanging flesh) and his dark hair and eyebrows.

He splashed cold water onto his face, wiped it with a towel.

He left the bathroom and sat on the bed for a few minutes. And then he thought of Elizabeth.

Elizabeth Schaefer. Thirty-three years old. Beautiful. With nothing to do for the weekend.

He looked down at his left hand. No wedding ring.

He shook his head.

Ridiculous, he thought. *You're being ridiculous. You have more important things to worry about.*

But Roger Schubert wasn't a middle-aged man any longer. He was young. And Elizabeth was alone for the weekend. That's what she had led him to believe, anyway.

Ridiculous, he thought.

But he didn't mean it.

Why not? he thought.

In his wallet, he had a *Weekend* phone list that included home phone numbers.

He dialed her number.

She answered the phone.

He said, in a voice that hadn't yet lost the energy and the optimism of youth, "May I speak to Elizabeth Schaefer?"

"Who is this?"

He could picture the cold suspicion in her beautiful, dark eyes.

He said, "My name is Buddy Schubert." (Roger's parents had always called him "Buddy" to distinguish him from his father, whose first name was also "Roger.") "My Uncle Roger suggested that I give you a call."

"Why?"

"Well, I'm on my way to Paris on business, but I've stopped off in New York City—just for the weekend—just to relax for a couple of days. And Uncle Roger said that, as always, there's a lot going on. And I said, could you stay in town and show me around? And he said he couldn't, but he suggested that you might have some free time."

There was no response.

"He said that there was a new Mary Cassatt show at the Metropolitan Museum of Art. And he gave me a couple of passes to the Boston Symphony concert tomorrow night: Seiji Ozawa, Shostakovich's Violin Concerto (I don't know who the soloist is), Beethoven's Seventh Symphony."

Finally, after another long pause, she said, "You can go alone."

Roger smiled when he heard Buddy say, "Maybe I'm crazy, but it isn't the same when I go alone. I don't really enjoy the experience unless I have someone to *share* it with, to *enjoy* it with, to *discuss* it with."

Pause, then, rather softly, "I—I know the feeling."

"I don't want you to get the wrong idea. This wouldn't be like a date. I'm very involved with someone back home—in Chicago. Maybe I should have said that first."

No response.

He said, "Uncle Roger said that you're interested in Mary Cassatt's work, and he was sure that the concert would appeal to you, too. After all, I'm not a stranger. Uncle Roger has a lot of respect for you. He wouldn't have given me your phone number unless he felt the same way about *me*."

"Why hasn't he ever mentioned you to me?"

"Uncle Roger is a very private man."

"I guess so. Well . . ."

"Please, Elizabeth. If you don't go with me, I'll just hang around the hotel all weekend. My fate is up to you."

"Well . . ."

"And dinner is on me, at any place of your choice."

She said, "Okay."

"You know, you might want to check me out before we actually meet tomorrow. Just to be sure that we're compatible."

"What do you mean?"

"Why don't you join me for dinner *tonight*—at my expense, of course."

"Tonight?"

"It doesn't have to be anything fancy. Maybe some neighborhood place that you like. Just to get to know each other."

"Why bother?"

"We can break the ice tonight and then, tomorrow, we don't have to waste a lot of time with that kind of stuff."

She said, "I get the feeling I'm being had."

"Elizabeth, that's not fair. We have dinner tonight. We go to the Mary Cassatt show tomorrow. Then dinner and the Boston Symphony concert. End of story. I fly off to Paris and we never see each other or speak to each other again for the rest of eternity. I repeat: End of story."

She said, under her breath, "End of story," then, "Do you like Italian food?"

"Love it."

"This is just what you said, a neighborhood place, okay?"

"Okay. Should I pick you up at your apartment?"

"No. What time is it? Twenty minutes to eight? I'll meet you there at eight thirty. It's called Marino's. It's at seventieth and Third Avenue. Take a cab."

"Marino's. Seventieth and Third at eight thirty. Thanks, Elizabeth."

"You're welcome."

He hung up the receiver and smiled.

He should buy a couple of ties (a young man's ties) she had never seen: there was a men's store in the hotel.

He'd better pay cash. He would get money from the ATM in the lobby.

I must be crazy, Roger thought.

But Buddy reassured him: "Relax. Enjoy the weekend."

He didn't take a cab. He took the subway—the Lexington Avenue Local from Grand Central to 68th Street—and walked the last three blocks to Marino's. As he approached the restaurant, he saw her sitting at an outdoor table. She was deep in conversation with one of the waiters.

She was still facing away from the street, still talking, when he stopped a few feet away from her and said, "Hello, Elizabeth."

She turned, examined his face for a moment, and said, tentatively, "Buddy?"

"That's me."

He extended his hand and she shook it.

She said, "How did you recognize me?"

It wasn't a casual question.

"Uncle Roger gave me a very accurate description of you."

She studied him more closely. "Jesus. You really look a lot like him. It's weird. I mean, not that there's anything weird about you. But seeing somebody who's a younger version of someone you know so well . . ."

"I hope that doesn't make you too uncomfortable."

He had chosen his words carefully: he knew that she wouldn't like him to think that anything made her uncomfortable—that is, gave him an advantage over her.

She straightened her back and the line of her mouth became tighter.

She said, coldly, "I'll get over it."

Roger smiled, not because of what she had said, but because he was free to sit there opposite her in a public place, and really look at her, admire her, and let her see that he admired her.

He asked, "Shall we order some wine? What are you in the mood for?"

She thought for a moment, then suggested an expensive Merlot. He ordered a bottle.

He said, "What a beautiful night."

"Yes, it is," she agreed, then added, after a polite pause, "Exactly how are you related to Roger?"

"I'm his brother's son."

"And you live in Chicago?"

"Yes. Always have."

"You said you were going to Paris on business. What business?"

"I'm a lawyer. I do a lot of work for international clients. But let's not talk shop tonight."

The wine arrived. The waiter uncorked it. Roger sampled it and approved.

When their glasses were filled, he raised his and said, "To a pleasant weekend—with a new friend."

She nodded, but limited her response: "To the weekend."

He said, "Uncle Roger tells me that you're a computer whiz."

She said, "Only in a sense. I mean, I'm not really a techie. But I'm very good at applications—at using computers as a tool."

"Was that what you studied in school?"

"God, no! My father would have killed me if I did anything like that. He's a history professor at Columbia. I was an English Lit major."

"Where?"

"I have a Bachelors and a Masters from Brown."

"How'd you learn about computers?"

"Just picked it up along the way."

The night air was cool and refreshing. The wine was smooth and friendly. The sounds of automobiles and the voices of passers-by blended into a blur of white noise. And there he was, completely at his ease on a busy, crowded New York City street, wearing a 35-year-old face, doing the boy-meets-girl thing with Elizabeth!

Oh, Roger, if they could see you now! (But, of course, they *could*.)

She asked him about his academic background. He decided that he had earned his undergraduate degree at the University of Chicago, and his law degree at Yale. He could see that she was impressed. *He* was, too.

He even toyed with the idea of winning a Rhodes Scholarship, but decided against it: he didn't know enough about Oxford University. Too bad.

She was getting slightly interested in him. Who could blame her?

She continued to grill him: "On the phone, you said that you're involved with someone. Tell me about her."

He wondered, *Should I challenge her, or give her the upper hand?*

He said, "She's not at all like you. She's not really interested in a career. She's very old-fashioned that way."

He could see the dawn of contempt in her eyes and the slight curl of her upper lip. (What a tasty-looking lip!)

He continued, "I met her at the University of Chicago. She was planning to be a psychologist, like your sister."

Elizabeth's eyes narrowed.

She said, "How do you know that my sister is a psychologist?"

The wine (plus those two Manhattans) had betrayed Roger.

How in hell do I know that Emily is a psychologist?

"You mentioned it before."

"No, I didn't."

"I guess Uncle Roger told me about her."

She raised one eyebrow, a perfect portrait of skepticism.

(*She should have been a cop*, he thought.)

She said, slowly, her tone ridiculing the idea, "Your Uncle Roger told you that my sister is a psychologist? Why the hell would he tell you *that*?"

He tried to smile away the problem: "Am I my uncle's keeper?"

She continued to scrutinize him. She was definitely not smiling.

He said, "Elizabeth, I don't know how I know. Maybe I'm psychic. What's the difference?"

The wine had apparently taken the edge off her mood, too.

She said, "I guess it doesn't matter."

"I agree. What matters is tonight and tomorrow."

She was just finishing her linguine with white clam sauce. She had built a pile of discarded shells in one corner of the plate—a tombstone for the deceased clams. The epitaph had almost read, "R.I.P. Roger Schubert *aka* Buddy, The Great Impostor."

He said, "Would you like dessert and coffee?"

She shook her head.

He said, "Me, neither. Would you like to take a walk? It's too nice a night to waste."

As they began to walk along Third Avenue (she chose the direction), he extended his arm and she linked her arm in his.

At first, they talked about tomorrow night's concert. Then they talked about Mary Cassatt and Paris (where Cassatt had lived and worked). Elizabeth window-shopped at a couple of clothing stores. They spent a few minutes debating the merits of a painting in the window of an antique store.

He asked, "Do you enjoy the work you do at *Weekend*? Is that what you always want to do?"

"I don't know. When I was at Brown, I thought I was going to teach in college, like my father. And maybe write."

"What made you change your mind?"

"I really didn't like the academic world. And I don't think I have the right temperament for teaching. Most people are too goddamn stupid to learn anything, anyway. Why bother trying to teach them?"

"So you're not too big on compassion, huh?"

"I guess not. My sister Emily is the good one. She always sympathizes with the underdog. I don't. I'm like my father, I guess."

"Is she like your mother?"

When she answered him, he felt her arm tighten around his, and her voice sounded smaller, almost like the voice of child.

She said, "Yes, she's like my mother. But she's stronger. Much stronger. She wouldn't let anyone control her life. She's her own person."

Roger didn't pursue the subject, but now he knew why Elizabeth never talked about her mother.

Suddenly she said, "I'm tired. I'm very tired. I need some sleep."

The tension in her arm diminished.

"Let me take you home."

She stopped in front of an apartment building they had just reached and said, "This *is* my home."

He smiled and said, "So you've been steering us here all along. Very clever."

She smiled, too.

He said, "Shall we start with brunch tomorrow, at about eleven?"

She nodded, said, "I'm in Apartment eight-G. Good night, Buddy."

He watched Elizabeth Schaefer walk away from him.

The first night of the weekend was over.

He had always pictured her apartment as neat, orderly, smartly decorated, and not very comfortable. It was quite the opposite.

The furniture was relaxed and not particularly elegant. Although the living room/dining room was spacious, it was no match for the avalanche of books, magazines and CDs that filled every shelf and overflowed onto every available surface, including the kitchen counter. In one corner of the living room, the screen of her PC peered out timidly from jagged piles of papers and folders. Groups of framed posters and watercolors crowded the walls. Several unframed prints leaned against the coffee table.

He thought, *Thank God her bedroom door is closed!*

However, she looked lovely—an island of calm in a sea of chaos. She was wearing a cool, sleeveless, pale-flowered dress. Her thick, dark hair was still slightly wet from the shower, like grass in morning dew. Her face and her arms still showed the gentle traces of the Provençal sun.

He said, "You look—great."

"Thanks." She inspected him and said, "Same suit. New tie."

"Oh, I didn't tell you: most of my luggage got lost on the way here. I just have my carry-on bag with me."

"My God."

"Well, the good news is: they found my stuff—in New Orleans."

"Jesus Christ!"

"It's on the way to Kennedy Airport, even as we speak. I told them to keep it there and I would pick it up on Sunday, when I leave. So this suit is all I've got, I'm afraid."

"I'll live."

They had brunch in another neighborhood place. She was very quiet during the meal, but she had a healthy appetite.

He followed her lead, not saying much, enjoying his coffee, enjoying the lines and colors and shades of her, the light and shadow.

She insisted that they take a taxi to the Metropolitan. "We have a long day ahead of us. Don't worry, I love to walk. I promise that we'll walk to Lincoln Center."

For Roger, the Mary Cassatt Show was really the Elizabeth Schaefer Show. He watched her react to the paintings.

Little Girl in a Blue Armchair—an awkwardly posed, dreamy child, sprawled out on a luxurious chair in a large, dark room, her dog curled up on another chair opposite her.

Elizabeth: "Portrait of Elizabeth as a kid. Alone. Never where I should be. But, of course, I didn't have a dog. My father said, 'If you want a dog, you have to walk him when it rains and snows. *I* won't.' As you would say, 'End of story.'"

Young Woman in Black—a hard-edged portrait of a self-assured, self-confident woman.

Elizabeth: "Now there's someone who does her own thing, goes her own way."

As he watched her, she stood a little straighter in front of the painting and tilted her head back, at the same arrogant angle as the Young Woman.

She virtually ignored all of the mother-and-child paintings—and there were many of them—except for *Woman and Child Driving*. Three figures in a horse-drawn carriage: a woman sits uneasily, the reins and whip held tightly, as if she isn't really in control; a little girl clutches the side of the carriage, staring ahead fearfully; a third figure (a servant? a footman?) rides on the rear of the carriage, behind the others, looking backwards, rather than forward.

Elizabeth: "The three of them *seem* to be together, but they're not. Scary little group, huh? How many families are like that? Everyone looking in a different direction, everyone seeing things from a different angle. Why is the mother so unsure of herself? What is that little girl afraid of? Does she think her mother is too weak to handle the carriage? Or is the kid just nervous about everything? It's really a nasty little scene."

Elizabeth moved through the exhibit erratically, rather than methodically. She doubled back and revisited some paintings, moved past others quickly and carelessly, and elbowed slower-moving museum-goers out of her way.

As Roger watched her plow through the galleries, he was reminded of her living room: chaos, disorder, a flood of unclassified, unsorted ideas.

But what's at the core of all that disorder? he wondered.

When they left the Metropolitan Museum, they walked south on Central Park West. It was a perfect Saturday in June and the streets were pleasantly crowded and noisy.

He said, "What do you think of my uncle?"

"*Think* of him?" she stalled, as she tried to decide how to respond.

"Well, he says some very nice things about you. But I always find him kind of—boring. You know: 'In *my* day, yaddah, yaddah, yaddah . . .'"

"He doesn't do much of that with me. He's a terrific editor. A good writer, too. And I don't really think he's that boring, considering his age. And he's a very good listener."

He thought, *With you, my dear, he'd better be*.

He asked, "What do you two talk about?"

She smiled.

"Me," she admitted.

"What do you mean?"

"Well, I always tell him about my problems, my boyfriends. I tell him just about everything. I like to use him as a sounding board. As an advisor. Not that I pay much attention to his advice, but that's the best part of it: he's a little bit like my father, except that I can ignore him. What could be more enjoyable than that?"

Roger laughed.

She said, "I think he enjoys it, too—playing that part. And I'm sure he doesn't take it very seriously, either. We get along well."

Roger decided to probe a little: maybe, as Buddy, he could get away with it.

He said, "I'd be interested in hearing about the men in your life."

She shook her head and frowned.

"That doesn't compute," she said.

"Why not? I'm just a ship, passing in the night. Before you know it, I'll be gone forever."

"So why should I tell you anything?"

"Sometimes it feels good to unload on a stranger—you know, like somebody you sit next to on an airplane."

She walked over to the low stone-and-concrete wall that bordered the park, and leaned against it. Roger followed her and did the same.

"You're a lot nosier than your uncle."

He shrugged.

She added, "For some strange reason, I almost trust you. And I don't trust anybody."

"You trust my uncle, don't you?"

She nodded. "Maybe."

He waited a couple of beats and then said, "Is there anyone special in your life right now?"

"No."

"How come?"

"Frankly, I'm beginning to wonder if there's anyone special out there at all. I haven't had much luck lately."

"You mean, you had more luck in the past?"

"Yes, I did. I was even engaged a couple of years ago."

"But you decided not to go through with it."

"No, *he* did."

Roger could see, immediately, that she regretted what she had said. The equilibrium between her and "Buddy" had shifted: she was suddenly more vulnerable.

She said, "Well, anyway, that's history."

He didn't respond quickly. He let the echo of her words fade into the background of traffic noise and passing conversations.

And when he spoke, it was really Roger who said, "I know I've only just met you but, for what it's worth, you don't seem to relax very much. You're always on guard. Or on edge. And I sense a lot of anger in you. Is it just that you're not comfortable with me, or is that a kind of—problem for you?"

She looked at him through an icy curtain. The revelations were apparently over.

She said, "I have a shrink in the family. I don't need any amateur psychoanalysis. Let's walk."

"I'm sorry. Will you forgive me?"

"Sure."

They passed a deformed beggar in a wheel chair.

She turned away from the beggar and said, "I hate ugliness. And pity is even worse."

There was an odd mixture of fear and anger in her voice.

He tried to steer them back to safer ground.

He said, "So you are your own favorite topic, eh?"

"I'm selfish, I guess. Not in the sense that I want what other people have. I just want to . . ."

She couldn't find an end for the sentence.

He said, "Be happy?"

"It sounds awfully dumb when you say it that way."

"How would *you* say it?"

"I don't want to answer to anyone else. I don't want to compromise. I don't want anyone setting limits on what I can do or say or be."

"Those are all negatives. Don't, don't, don't. That's the anger I was talking about. You sound like you're at war."

"War is hell," she said, softly.

He assumed that she was being honest with him because she knew that they would never see each other again.

It was still a pleasure to look at her—a flash of pale flowers, sun-touched skin, dark hair and eyes: beautiful. But he was beginning to reach beyond the disorder and the chaos: *not* so beautiful.

At dinner they debated the relative merits of Shostakovich and Prokofiev without reaching any conclusion. This led to a discussion of the relative merits of symphonic music and chamber music, with equally inconclusive results.

This led to dessert and coffee.

Their conversation—their relationship—had already established a pattern. She was friendly, but distant. She had inadvertently told him too much about herself, and she wouldn't make that same mistake again.

Because of Buddy, Roger knew her better now. Much better.

At the concert, Roger began to feel very tired—tired of being Buddy, tired of the sound of his own voice, tired of being young again.

And he had to admit that he was also tired of Elizabeth Schaefer.

He didn't know what he had expected her to be. Free-spirited? Exciting? Uninhibited?

That's not what he saw when he looked at her now. He saw a Mary Cassatt painting of a little girl sprawled awkwardly on a luxurious chair, alone, or fearfully hanging on to a carriage that was going nowhere.

He closed his eyes.

The music cleared his mind. The youthful tension in him began to relax. He thought of his wife, his sons, his grandchildren.

He remembered how difficult it was to be young. This weekend had reminded him of that.

He knew that by the time he got home on Sunday morning, he would be fifty-seven years old again.

And he knew that, on Monday morning, he might still wish he could touch her dark hair or kiss her mouth, and now that wish would be linked to a fragment of memory.

To Buddy, Elizabeth Schaefer was a woman.

To Roger, she would always remain a beautiful illusion.

But, he thought, *without illusions, life would be a very dreary place.*

DAWN

At about seven o'clock in the evening on a chilly Valentine's Day, Adam Stein got a call from Pittsburgh, the city where he was born. He listened for a minute or two, asked a few questions, said, "I'll be there tomorrow morning," and hung up the receiver.

He had been eating dinner, so he had answered the extension in the kitchen. The phone was on a small table in the corner of the room. After the call, he continued to sit in the chair by that table, looking down at his hands in his lap, as if they were blank pages he was stubbornly trying to read.

An icy breeze whispered through the branches of the trees in the back yard. A brazen, yellow moon, gleaming harshly in the clear sky, stared at him through the window.

He sat in the quiet house, trying to understand what he had just heard.

He reached for the phone, lifted the receiver again, put it to his ear and dialed.

A man's voice said, "Hello."

"Steven, it's Adam. Can I speak to Marcie?"

She was his ex-wife.

Steven didn't answer him, but called her name and said, "Adam's on the phone."

Marcie's voice had a familiar, guarded edge when she asked, "What's up, Adam?"

"Danny is dead."

She inhaled sharply and said, in a smaller, thinner voice, "What happened?"

"One of those kids killed him—for a credit card. The kid wanted to get flowers for his girlfriend, so he killed Danny. And, of course, the kid was spaced out on something and he went right to a flower shop and used the card and the cops caught him. He confessed. Some stupid, drugged-out bastard killed my brother—who was trying to help him, who gave him a place to sleep, fed him."

"I'm so sorry, Adam. I know how much you love him. I love him, too."

"I told him this would happen. He would bring these kids home—to our house, the house where we grew up. When I went to see him a couple of months ago, they were all over the place, sleeping on couches, on cots. The place was like a dormitory for losers. And he joked around with them and smiled at them and held their hands and loved them. I told him this would happen."

"I'm so sorry. Is there anything I can do?"

"No. It's just . . . You were the only one I could tell. The only one who knew him."

She was crying.

He said, "A policeman called. Danny wanted to be buried near our parents. He bought a plot alongside them. I said I would come to identify him and claim the body and make the arrangements tomorrow morning."

"Are you flying there?"

"No, I'll drive. It's maybe seven or eight hours to Pittsburgh. There won't be much traffic now."

"Maybe it would be better to go by plane. The way you feel, maybe it's too far to drive."

"No. I won't be able to sleep tonight, anyway. I'll get coffee, something to eat on the Pike. I want time to think. I don't want to get there too fast. I'll be there in the morning."

"Would you like me to go with you?"

"Thank you, Marcie. I'd rather be alone. Thank you."

"We'll be at the funeral. Make sure you call us with all the information."

"Sure. Goodbye."

Adam was thirty-eight years old. At seventeen, he had left Pittsburgh to go to Boston University. He did his graduate work in history at Harvard and, with his Ph.D. in hand, taught there for a couple of years. When he met Marcie, she was an undergraduate in one of his classes. After she earned her degree, they were married and he finally landed a better job as an associate professor of history at Fairfield University in Connecticut. She worked at a Stamford public relations agency as an account executive. They lived in Fairfield.

After three years, the marriage ended. They had no children. Adam still lived in the house that he and Marcie had bought.

He had driven from Fairfield to Pittsburgh many times, at first to see his mother and father, as well as Danny. Both of his parents had died more than ten years ago, a few months apart. As a social worker, Danny didn't make much money, so he had continued to live with his parents, and he had kept the house after they died. He had never been married.

Danny was three years younger than Adam. A girl, Amanda, was born after Danny, but she died when she was eight.

Now there was no one left but Adam.

An hour later, he was driving south on I-95 at sixty miles an hour, staying in the right lane so the faster traffic could pass him.

The bare limbs of the roadside trees shivered in the winter wind.

He thought, *It was kind of Marcie to offer to come with me. She loves—she loved Danny, but who didn't?*

And it wasn't because Danny was a gentle man.

He once said, "People don't want to be judged. They don't want to be forgiven. They want to be understood."

Even as a child, Danny almost never asked, "Why?"

He asked, "What can I do about it?"

When Adam and Marcie separated, Danny wanted to know what he could do to bring them back together.

"Nothing," Adam said. "It isn't her fault, it's mine. I'm not good at intimacy."

Danny shook his head. "You shouldn't lock yourself into categories. I'm not this, I'm that. She's not this, she's that."

"But I *am*, and she *is*."

Danny laughed. But he really couldn't help.

Adam thought, *Judgment. That's how I made my reputation.*

As an historian, it was his intense, ruthless pursuit of the truth, his refusal to accept any authority but his own judgment that had attracted favorable, as well as hostile, attention to his articles and books.

He had written, "The truth is always elusive and, when you track it down and corner it, it is never satisfying, and never what you expected. If it is, you are deceiving yourself. Great men are hollow. Great victories are empty. Great civilizations are corrupt. Great revolutions spawn new tyranny, even if it is only the tyranny of mediocrity. You may love the truth, but it will not return your love."

What did he know about love?

He knew that he loved Danny. He knew that he had loved Amanda, too.

She was a fragile child. Her smile was serene and comforting. She rarely felt the sharp edge of Mother's wit, and she could even make Father laugh.

When Adam looked back on his childhood, he remembered two sets of parents, separated by a wall of ice.

On the far side of that wall, his mother was an aggressive, clever woman, small and narrow, sinewy and quick. Her humor was usually at other peoples' expense. She had been a high school math teacher, who had left her job to raise her children and she dominated the dinner table as if it were her classroom. (Physically, Danny resembled her.)

Father was thickset, somber and laconic. He was a senior partner of a successful accounting firm. He repeated one lesson to his children, over and over, in a thousand different ways: "They're all out to cheat you. Don't let them get away with it." And his eyes, deep-set and dark, seemed always to be searching for "them"—the cheaters.

Then, suddenly, Amanda died, killed accidentally by a car in the school parking lot. The wall of ice froze into place. Mother became quiet and thoughtful. She lost her edge, her wit, her interest in other people, including her husband and her sons. She did everything she had done before, but by rote.

Father no longer searched for "them." They had cheated him, at last, and they had gotten away with it.

Adam was angry about Amanda's death. He asked, "Why?"

Danny, only eleven years old, tried to ease his parents' pain. He couldn't reach them, neither of them.

They hadn't been affectionate before Amanda's death; now they were distant, shadowy, out of focus.

Danny never blamed them. Adam did.

Danny said, "They're terrible parents. They always were, but they do the best they can. They're limited. They never trusted the world, and neither do you. We have to try to help them."

"I don't want to help them. I don't care about them."

Danny cared. Danny tried.

When Danny was in college, his freshman English professor asked the students in the class to write an essay about the worst thing that had ever happened to them. Danny didn't always follow directions. He often created his own curriculum and he usually got away with it.

Instead of writing an essay, he wrote a sonnet about Amanda's death. It wasn't a great poem, but it said everything he had to say about her, without bitterness.

Tomorrow's never

When can I ride up front with you? she'd always
Ask. When you don't need a booster seat,
He'd say. And think: Don't hurry growing. Seize the days
Of child's-eye views, kaleidoscopic, sweet
But fearful, too, when we seem giants, towering high,
Your judges, juries, saying Yes or No
To instincts, fantasies, and rarely telling Why.
We help them learn; they lose their sunrise glow.
She never lost it, or her silvery voice,
Still small and musical. I hear it yet,
Pretending, laughing. If I had my choice,
It is a sound I'd wish I could forget.
At eight, she died: too brief a history.
Tomorrow's never where we think it's going to be.

Now, on a windy Valentine's-Day night, as he drove across the George Washington Bridge into New Jersey, toward a room where Danny's lonely body lay, Adam remembered his sister's death, his brother's sonnet, his mother's silence, his father's empty eyes.

Just past Allentown, Pennsylvania, he stopped at a service area for gas, then went into a Dunkin' Donuts for coffee and a muffin.

There was a young family sitting at a table nearby. The husband and wife were in their early thirties, attractive, dressed in expensive sports clothes. The man was holding a sleeping baby in one arm, while he drank his coffee and ate a donut with his free hand. The woman was having an animated conversation with their three-year-old daughter.

Adam tried to remember a moment like that in his own childhood. He couldn't. Although his father had sometimes held Amanda that way, they never sat together quietly, as a family, and shared their feelings. Mother didn't approve of feelings and Father kept his to himself. Danny would often try to break down the barriers, but he always failed. And Adam didn't really help him very much. He didn't want Mother to make fun of him, or Father to disapprove of him.

Eventually, Adam stopped trying to love his parents. It was easier after Amanda died. In fact, he had the feeling that they loved her more *after* she died than when she was still alive, maybe because it was easier for them to love a memory that could never grow up to disappoint them.

When Adam met Marcie, he was impressed with her intelligence, but he was uncomfortable with her warmth. She was so at ease with herself and she said whatever came into her mind, whether it was clear or jumbled or a little of both. She didn't edit herself the way Adam did. He was always concerned about showing too much of himself, or saying something foolish, or being wrong.

He watched her the way he would watch a soaring bird in flight or a meteorite racing through the night sky.

When he asked her to marry him, he knew that it was a mistake.

He was right. He couldn't accustom himself to intimacy. He couldn't tolerate the naked hunger of sexuality that stripped him of his defenses.

He couldn't love Marcie. He tried, but love would have made him too vulnerable. He could be hurt. He could fail.

And if he did, he knew he would hear Mother laughing.

West of Harrisburg, he reached the Pennsylvania Turnpike. A few minutes later, he saw a young woman on the shoulder, sitting on a suitcase, trying to hitch a ride. A shabby old car was parked at a helpless angle behind her, leaning into a shallow ditch.

Adam didn't think that he should pick her up. But he was more tired than he had expected to be. The first rush of emotion had ebbed. Talking to someone would help keep him awake.

Adam slowed down and pulled over onto the shoulder just past her. He watched her approach his car in the side-view mirror. She opened the front door on the passenger side and stuck her head in.

"Thanks," she said.

When he saw her face, he felt a surge of anger.

She was probably eighteen or nineteen years old. Her short, blond hair was streaked with faded purple splotches and pulled into jagged spikes with a thick layer of mousse. She had a row of tiny gold rings in one ear and long gold crosses hung from each earlobe. Her left eyebrow was pierced with a gold post and a large, gold stud gleamed on the shell of one nostril.

He said, "Put your bag in the back seat."

She climbed into the front seat and slammed the door shut.

She was shivering and her teeth were chattering. She was wearing jeans and a T-shirt, with only a denim jacket to keep her warm on a February night. He almost felt sorry for her.

Then she looked at him and, when she did, he saw that her eyes were hollow and focused somewhere else. He recognized the addict's stare that he had seen so often in Danny's kids and in some of his students: a mixture of fear, ecstasy and emptiness.

That must have been the look in the eyes of the kid who had killed Danny. That look was the last thing Danny saw.

"Thanks," she said again.

He turned up the heat in the car.

He said, "Do you want to stop at a gas station and go back for your car?"

"No. It's dead. The guy who gave it to me said that it probably wouldn't make it to Pittsburgh."

He wondered if she had stolen the car.

"I'm going to Pittsburgh. I'll take you there."

He drove back onto the Turnpike. He suddenly felt clear-headed and energetic. Refreshed.

She said, "I could give you a couple of bucks for gas."

"I don't need a couple of bucks."

"What *do* you want?" she asked, with an obvious inflection.

"Just someone to talk to. To keep me awake. I'm driving all night."

She folded her arms over her breast, hugging herself to generate heat.

She said, "Okay."

"What's your name?"

"Moonlight."

"Moonlight?"

"Right. Nice, huh?"

"Very nice. Where are you from?"

"Boston."

"Are you going to school?"

"No. I don't like school."

"What *do* you like?"

She laughed. "Just about everything else."

"Do your parents know where you are?"

"I don't have parents."

"Dead?"

"More or less. Are you a cop or something?"

"No. I'm a teacher."

"Just my fuckin' luck. So I've got to take a test all night?"

"I'm just making conversation. Remember, that's why I picked you up."

"Yeah, yeah. Okay, teacher, but why don't we talk about you."

"Sure."

"What's your name?"

"Adam."

"Where are you from?"

"Pittsburgh, originally. But now I live in Connecticut."

"Are you married?"

"No."

"You don't look like the bachelor type. Guys like you always get married."

"Maybe the exception proves the rule."

"What does that mean?"

"Never mind."

"My fuckin' teachers always talked like that."

"Did you finish high school?"

"No. I thought *I* was asking the questions."

"Sorry."

"What do you teach? Not sex education, I'll bet."

"History."

"Borrrring. Why are you going to Pittsburgh?"

"To visit family."

"Your parents?"

"No."

"Dead?"

"Yes."

"Do you miss them?"

"No."

"I don't miss mine, either. Well, I don't know who the hell my father was. Neither did my mother. She was a pain in the ass."

"You mean because she wanted you to go to school?"

Moonlight laughed.

She said, "Her? Are you kidding? All she wanted to do was get stoned and screw her latest boyfriend. She wouldn't give a shit if I jumped out the fuckin' window."

Adam almost began to sympathize with her, but he shrugged off the feeling.

He thought, *She killed Danny*.

She said, "I'm hungry. I'll pay for my own food. I'd love to have something to eat. Do you mind stopping for a few minutes?"

"No. There's a diner a few miles from here, just off the Pike. I've been there before."

"Thanks. Who are you going to see in Pittsburgh?"

"My brother."

"Is he a teacher, too?"

"No."

Adam thought, *He's someone who wasted his life trying to help people like you.*

He said, "Is it my turn again, yet? To ask the questions?"

"Does it have to be?"

"Yes."

"Shit. Go ahead."

"I'll tell you what: I'll give you a rest—until we get to the diner."

"I'm beginning to lose my appetite."

He almost laughed at that.

The waitress who took their orders looked at them disapprovingly and Adam didn't blame her. He might have been the girl's father, but the waitress doubted it and, to her, any other possibility was unpleasant or unthinkable.

Moonlight ordered a bacon cheeseburger deluxe and a vanilla malted. It was almost three-thirty in the morning, so Adam ordered scrambled eggs, hash browns, toast and coffee.

Moonlight was tired. They were sitting in a booth and she leaned her head back, rested it on the tall, upright back cushion of the seat and closed her eyes. He studied her face. If you looked past the hardware and the patches of purple hair and the mousse, you might call her pretty. She was tall and very slim. Her hands were clasped on the table in front of her. They were surprisingly delicate, long-fingered, graceful.

She said, "Something wrong with my hands?"

He looked up at her.

"No."

"So what are you staring at them for?"

"No reason. You ready for more questions?"

"Yes, teacher."

"Why are you going to Pittsburgh?"

"To meet a guy."

"Your boyfriend?"

"Sort of. My friend, anyway. He knows a lot of people there."

"What kind of people?"

Her eyes narrowed and she said, "*People* people."

"I understand."

"You don't understand shit. You think you do, but you don't."

"What don't I understand?"

"I just got out of rehab. I'm clean."

"For how long? A week? A month? And this friend of yours in Pittsburgh, is he clean, too?"

"What do you care?"

He paused, looked out the window. Even through the glass, the starlight was abnormally bright and brittle, as if the sky were a backdrop on a huge stage, exaggerating reality, rather than imitating it.

She said, "You sure you're not a cop? You ask questions like a cop."

"I'm just after the truth."

"Why does it matter whether I'm telling the truth or not? I could make up any fuckin' story I want to about my life. Shit, I'm not even sure that everything I remember really happened. I don't care. Maybe I made it *all* up."

He nodded. "Sometimes it feels that way, doesn't it?"

She recognized a different, distant sound in his voice and echoed it: "Yeah, it does."

"You think about the choices you made, and you wonder, if I had done this, or that, what would my life be like today. Better? Worse? Or maybe even the same."

"Sometimes you don't have any choices."

"You mean 'character is fate'?"

"Huh?"

He smiled. "We think we have lots of choices, but we really don't, because we're too afraid to pick some of them, or too weak, or whatever."

She nodded.

The waitress arrived with their food. She squinted her disapproval of them as she set the plates down.

After she left, Moonlight said, "I'm eating. No more talk, okay?"

She ate hungrily, noisily, happily.

Adam tried not to watch her.

He remembered a teenage girl Danny had introduced him to, a year or two ago. She had just come out of a drug rehab program and she was living at Danny's house.

"This is Eleanor," Danny said. "She's going to be a nurse. She's just applied for nursing school—and we're sure she'll be accepted."

Danny always said "we" when he meant "I." Adam knew that it wasn't humility: it was Danny's sense that we're all connected.

Eleanor was delicate and small-boned. Her eyes were large and dark and there was no hope in them, but she nodded as if she agreed with Danny.

Danny put his arm around her and said, "We're very proud of Eleanor. She can beat the devil."

But a few weeks later, the devil beat Eleanor, killing her with an overdose.

And, Adam thought, the devil would beat Moonlight, too.

He said, "How did you come up with Moonlight?"

"It's my name."

"I doubt it."

"So doubt it. What do I care?"

"How many times have you been in rehab?"

"Why the hell did you pick me up? You're about as friendly as a snake."

"I told you: I wanted to talk to someone so I could stay awake."

"I should have *walked* to Pittsburgh."

"You only have to stay with me for another few hours. Then you'll never see me again."

"'Never' isn't long enough."

He said, "Do you have AIDS yet?"

She sighed and shook her head.

She said, "They tested me at the rehab center. Don't look so disappointed. Keep the faith and maybe I'll die young, anyway."

"It's only a matter of time."

"Jesus, you are one cheerful fuck."

"I know the pattern. I've seen it a hundred times. The story is always the same."

"Not my story."

"Why not?"

"Because *you're* not going to write my story: *I* am."

He shrugged. "I won't ask any more questions."

"Good. And I'll pay for my own food."

"No, it's all right."

"I want to."

"Save your money."

"Jesus Christ, you're a pain in the ass."

When they got back on the Turnpike, they drove in silence for almost two hours. Adam kept thinking about Danny's body, waiting for him, cold and alone. He would never speak to Danny again, or smile at him, or tell him a joke. Adam tried to imagine the world without his brother. And then he thought of the boy who had killed him. And the anger began to churn in him, until he could taste the acid in his throat.

Moonlight had catnapped at intervals. He looked over at her and she was awake.

He said, "I told you I was going to Pittsburgh to see my brother. That isn't the whole truth. I'm going there to identify him and claim his body. He was killed yesterday."

"In an accident?"

"No. He was a social worker. He tried to help kids like you—drug addicts, prostitutes, losers. And one of them killed him—for a credit card. Maybe it was your boyfriend. Who knows?"

She whispered, "Shit."

"He was going to save people. Save the children. Lead them into the Promised Land. So one of them killed him."

He knew that he wanted her to feel guilty, as if her guilt could diminish his own. He had never cared about other people. He had never been able to love anyone—except his brother and sister. He lived a comfortable, safe life, critiquing the work of other scholars, teaching his own narrow, parasitic, personal version of history, risking nothing, helping no one.

And Danny was dead.

Adam said, "How old were you when you began taking drugs?"

She answered mechanically, as if she were just trying to get it over with, "Twelve, thirteen. My mother was the one who started me."

"Just one big, happy family, huh?"

"Yeah."

"You really have no idea who your father was?"

"What's the difference? I made believe that he was dead. Maybe he is."

"Did your mother work?"

"Sometimes. As a waitress, or an office temp. She'd collect a few checks and then quit and spend it all."

"On drugs."

"No, on encyclopedias. We had Britannicas up the ass."

"And . . ."

She said, very softly, "Leave me alone, will you?"

"Who started you on sex?"

"One of the guys who lived with my mother."

"How old were you then?"

"Fourteen, I think."

"Did she know?"

"Sure. It made her feel less up tight, knowing I was into the same shit she was."

"Were you ever a prostitute?"

"Sure. Men, women, you name it, I did it."

She repeated, "I did it," but it had a different sound, confessional, rather than defiant.

The tone of her voice reminded Adam of what Danny had said, that people don't want to be forgiven; they want to be understood.

He was in no mood to do either.

He said, "I'll take you to your friend in Pittsburgh, like I promised, but first you've got to go somewhere with me."

"You're not starting to get weird now, are you?"

He shook his head.

She said, "You signing me up for college, or something?"

"No, but you could call it an educational visit, if you like."

"Christ!"

"It won't take long, I promise. And it's in a public place."

"That's doesn't mean shit. I've done some disgusting things in public places."

"I'm sure you have."

"Thanks for believing in me."

He smiled.

After a long beat, she asked, "What's your brother's name?"

"Danny."

"Were you real close to him?"

He hesitated.

Then he thought, *Telling her should be easy. She's a stranger*. Besides, it would be better if she knew about Danny before they got there. It would be much more educational.

"Danny was close to everybody. It came naturally to him. I'm not like that."

"No shit!"

"If he met you like this, he'd make sure you had a place to crash tonight—a safe place—and a hot meal. And he'd tell you what a great kid you are."

"I guess the wrong brother died, huh?"

"I guess so."

He had the feeling that she was watching him. He glanced over at her and, when he did, she smiled at him, not as if she were mocking him, but as if she were reassuring him.

"I can't believe you aren't married."

"I was, for a few years."

"Aha! Who broke it up?"

"I did."

"Why?"

"I wasn't good at it."

She laughed in advance and said, "Maybe you didn't practice enough."

Adam shrugged and said, "I don't think I'd ever get the hang of it."

"Any kids?"

"No."

"But you teach kids."

"In college. If they want to learn, fine, but that's up to them. It's not my problem."

"Remind me never to take your course. You must be a pretty shitty teacher."

"You're right. But I publish a lot of articles and books. I'm sort of famous, in a way. So it doesn't matter how well I teach. I'm the kind of star a school is always looking for."

"I thought teachers are supposed to be good at teaching."

"You thought wrong. A college is a business. And people like me are good for business."

"You said you weren't good at marriage. And you aren't good at teaching. And you also said you weren't good at being close to people, like your brother. But you're good for business. Shit, I guess that's better than nothing."

He didn't respond.

She asked, "It *is* better than nothing, isn't it?"

He thought, *Is she judging me?*

He asked, "Are you judging me? You?"

"No. I'm just looking for the truth."

He shook his head and said, "You think that's funny, don't you?"

"Funnier than shit. Jesus Christ, I do what I'm good at, and you do what you're good at. That's what everybody does, right?"

He didn't answer her.

He didn't look at her.

He drove through the cold, February night and listened to the icy wind rush past the car, whispering, moaning, mourning.

When he drove up to the Morgue, it was a few minutes after nine a.m.

Moonlight said, "Shit. I'm not going in there."

"I drove you all the way to Pittsburgh. I fed you. I let you make fun of me. Do me a favor. Come with me."

"I don't want to see no dead bodies."

"It'll only take a few minutes. It'll make it easier for me if you come with me."

"I don't give a shit if it's easier for you."

"Please. Come with me."

She searched his face.

She said, "What's the game? You trying to make me feel guilty? I didn't do anything."

"Come with me."

"This is fuckin' unfair."

"It won't take long. And then I'll take you to your friend. I promise."

"Shit."

She went with him.

She stood a few feet from him, her hands deep in her jeans' pockets, as Adam went through the formalities of identifying himself. The policeman called someone and hung up the phone. A few minutes later, the phone rang, the policeman picked it up, said, "Okay" and hung it up again.

He gestured to Adam and said, "Follow me."

Adam turned to Moonlight and repeated the gesture and also said, "Follow me."

They walked through a steel double door, down a long, grey-walled corridor, through another steel double door into a high-ceilinged room where the air felt like the chilly breeze from a refrigerator when you open it on a hot, sticky day.

A sheet covered a body on a steel gurney. Adam moved very close to the gurney and pulled her along with him. The policeman uncovered the face of the corpse.

Adam thought, *He looks so small. So small. The way he looked when he was a little boy, fast asleep, in the bed next to mine*. Adam would watch him and wonder what he was dreaming, and what he would become. And this was what he had become. A cold, silent shadow of himself. All the kindness, all the love, all the possibilities, were frozen like the wall that their parents had built when Amanda was killed.

They were *all* behind that wall now. And he might as well be.

Adam said, "Yes, that's my brother Danny."

The policeman said, "Daniel Stein?"

"Yes, Daniel Stein."

Then Adam confirmed his brother's address.

The policeman said that he should fill out a form, so the funeral parlor could pick up the body.

Moonlight said, "Can we go?"

The policeman covered Danny's face with the sheet and said, "I have his effects up at the desk."

Adam didn't cry. He and Moonlight returned to the desk with the policeman. Adam filled out the form. The policeman gave him a large manila envelope.

Adam said, "Thank you," and then he and Moonlight left the Morgue and went back to his car.

He didn't look in the envelope. He put it in the back seat with her suitcase.

He asked, "Where should I drop you off?"

"Why the hell did I have to come here with you?"

"I told you. It was educational."

"Well, you know me: I'm hopeless. I didn't learn anything."

"Sure you did. You learned what a good man looks like when he's been cheated out of his life."

"That's some fucking lesson."

"You know, you're what Danny was trying to save. Kids who shoot up—and fuck up. You're what he died for."

Adam hadn't started the engine of the car yet, but his hands gripped the wheel tightly, so tightly that his forearms ached.

"I told him a thousand times that no one could help those kids. I told him that they were just taking advantage of him. He gave them food and comfort and a place to crash and they stayed until they were strong enough to go out and fuck up all over again. In and out of rehab. In and out of jail. In and out of hospitals. And he was always there for them. For you."

His head throbbed with the furious, fierce rhythm of his heartbeat.

He said, "And one of them was there for *him*. I know how he felt when he died: not angry, not afraid. Just disappointed. Disappointed."

He heard something that sounded like laughter. He looked at her. She was sobbing. Tears streamed down her face.

She said, very softly, very coldly, "You stupid bastard. You stupid fuckin' bastard. Do you think I *want* this life?"

His anger dissipated suddenly, like smoke in an icy wind.

Adam watched the morning traffic move through the streets.

The sky to the east was bright now. The sun had erased the stars but he could still see the ghost of the moon, hovering like a memory of night.

They sat in silence for a few minutes. He tried to think clearly, but he found it hard to concentrate on anything.

He saw Danny's face again, not the way it was now, but the way it used to be. Gentle, forgiving.

Finally he said, "Why do you keep doing the same things, over and over again? The men, the drugs, all that crap."

"Because that's what I am. That's all I am."

"Maybe you can be someone else."

She turned to him and asked, "Can *you* be someone else? You can't be."

"How old are you?"

"Seventeen."

"Seventeen."

The tension seeped out of him. He leaned back, breathed deeply.

For the first time that night, he really smiled.

He said, "Listen, don't meet your boyfriend today."

"Why not? I think you're getting weird."

"No. I'm not getting weird. Let's go to Danny's house—it's the house where I grew up. You'll stay there while I take care of Danny's funeral."

"Why should I stay there?"

"After the funeral, I want you to come back to Connecticut with me."

She said, "Oh, shit, I've heard that song before."

"No, no, no, you're wrong. I have some friends—a married couple. They have a room they'll rent you. I'll take care of it. Money's no problem. I expect you to pay me back when you can."

"What the hell are you talking about?"

"They're very nice people. And I'll get help for you."

"I don't need help."

"At the university, there are special programs, and there are plenty of people there to help you. Please, let me do this."

"Do *what*? What are you, all of a sudden: my best friend?"

"Maybe."

"All of a sudden, you forgive me?"

He shook his head.

"No. I have nothing to forgive you for."

"Why should I believe you? Why would you want to help me?"

"Hey, I may not be any good at it. I never tried it before."

"You sure you're not crazy?"

"If I'm crazy, why would you believe me if I tell you that I'm *not*?"

She laughed.

He said, "Let's try it. Let's see what happens."

She said, "I think it would be a mistake to try it."

"Fairfield is a nice town. You'll like it."

"Shit. I don't know."

He waited for her answer.

She said, "I must be a fuckin' maniac. But, okay, why not."

She shook her head a few times, as if she were disagreeing with herself.

He said, "Okay."

He started the car, but he stayed in Park.

He said, "Before we go any further, there's one thing you have to tell me: your name. Your *real* name."

She turned toward him. The fresh light of the new sun, rising behind them, touched her face, glowed in the tears on her cheeks, sparkled from the golden slivers in her ear, her nose and her brow.

Her eyes watched him cautiously.

"Dawn," she said.

WHEELER-DEALER

If I told you that my boss was Morton MacNeil Wheeler, that name would undoubtedly conjure up a potpourri of misinformation and disinformation—half-digested fragments of TV documentaries, tabloid exposés, *Fortune* and *Forbes* magazine profiles, and Internet gossip.

And nothing could please my boss more than his bizarre public image: the brilliant, unpredictable, zany, lascivious—not to mention "filthy rich"—hermit.

By nurturing this image—which, by the way, is more accurate than he'd like to admit—Wheeler has transformed his idiosyncratic behavior into a valuable business asset. And, take my word for it, Business (with a capital "B") is what Morton MacNeil Wheeler is all about.

He is, in fact, precisely what *Forbes* magazine called him: "America's supreme Wheeler-Dealer."

Negotiating with him is quite an experience. For one thing, you never actually see him in person. If you're lucky, he may present himself to you via audiotape. If you're *very* lucky, he may deign to converse with you via Speakerphone. But he never actually gets involved in the nitty-gritty negotiations. He leaves that to a team of go-betweens, including yours truly,

Jason Greene, an impoverished lawyer who became a prosperous hand-puppet.

Hand-puppet? you say. *But aren't you negotiating multimillion dollar deals?*

Not really. You see, Wheeler's "team" was just a scrim of empty suits. As long as the stage lights were off, you couldn't see through us. The fact is, he told us what to say, how to say it, what to offer, what to demand. We were actors in a successful soap opera: well-paid and looking forward to a long run. And the characters we played were shallow stereotypes.

That sounds pretty grim, doesn't it?

But in my salad days, when I was a young, idealistic lawyer (with a JD from Columbia) who cared about people, who fought on the barricades for the oppressed, the poor, the voiceless—guess what? I was as oppressed, as poor, and as voiceless as they were.

My wife got tired of living hand to mouth. She left, divorced me and married a podiatrist. (I guess you could call that a corny ending.)

Finally, a few years later, I got tired. My idealism curdled. My nobility faded.

I admit it. I'm not a saint. I wanted the good things in life. I sold out. And Wheeler was buying.

I was interviewed by his Number One, as Wheeler called him (he must have seen too many Charlie Chan movies), Jethro Kelly, an accountant who looked like an aging nightclub bouncer. My Columbia law degree was helpful: Wheeler was proud of his Columbia BA (Class of 1930). My lack of a wife was also a plus. Wheeler preferred employees who had no strong emotional ties. "Married to the job" was a phrase that pleased him. My newly discovered greed didn't hurt, either.

Number One hired me. And my life became totally unplanned and chaotic. I could be called at two a.m. and told that a ticket was waiting for me at Kennedy Airport. I would be on the next plane to Denver or San Diego or London or Oahu. (Wheeler owned a luxury hotel chain and maintained a penthouse apartment in his best hotel in every major city.) When I picked up the ticket, I would also receive a locked attaché case with information to study en route. I learned my lines, played my role, and waited for the next call to arms.

In the beginning, for more than a year, I never saw Wheeler himself. Then, one icy November evening, I got a call that sent me to Paris, but there was no attaché case waiting for me at the airport. There was just a brief note from Number One that said, "The Man Himself wants to meet you," or words to that effect.

Although I flew first class, the flight was bumpy and uncomfortable. I didn't sleep at all, but I downed several glasses of wine. I was greeted at the Paris airport by a supercilious chauffeur with a sinister smile that chilled me to the marrow. The limousine was as cold as a refrigerator. By the time I reached the door of Wheeler's Parisian penthouse, I felt like a frozen side of beef in a meat locker.

Number One met me at the door and ushered me into the living room, which was dimly lit by a single standing lamp in the far corner and the dying embers in the fireplace. The hot, humid air of the apartment was like a warm, tropical storm washing over me. (Wheeler swore that he could only survive in moist heat. "I'm a lizard," he would say. "I generate no heat of my own.")

Number One said, "Mr. Wheeler. Jason Greene."

Then he left.

I couldn't see anyone else in the room. I walked toward the fireplace, peering into the darkness. A tall, slim figure suddenly emerged from the shadows, startling me. A huge hand extended itself and a soft, rasping voice said, "Jason."

I shook the hand (it was moist and bony) and answered, "Mr. Wheeler."

He gestured toward the couch near the window and asked, "Would you like a drink? Orange juice? Cranberry?"

"Cranberry juice, thank you."

He disappeared into the shadows again. My eyes began to accustom themselves to the darkness. I could see him filling a glass with ice cubes and pouring my drink.

After he gave me the glass, he sat down in a plush armchair across from me and lit a cigar. I sipped the juice and had a moment to study him.

Morton MacNeil Wheeler was quite tall—six foot three or four—and very lean. I knew that he was in his sixties, but he moved like an athlete, or a predator: silently, fluidly, almost sinuously. He was dressed in black—a black shirt and slacks, and a black sport jacket. His thin, gray hair was cut very short. His face was almost skeletal: you could trace the outline of his skull beneath the skin. His eyes were large and dark, and set deep in their sockets. His teeth were huge and too white. His nose was long, razor thin and straight. And his voice was very soft and rough, like the sound of fine sandpaper on smooth wood.

"It's a pleasure to meet you at last, Jason."

"My pleasure, sir."

"I've been following your work very closely. You've been doing an excellent job. Excellent."

"Thank you, sir."

He puffed on his cigar and the smoke he exhaled hung in the humid air like a dialogue balloon in a comic strip.

"You're ready for bigger things. I want you to take the lead on a couple of new projects."

"Thank you, sir."

"More money," he added.

"Thank you, sir."

He uncoiled from his chair and began to move around the room, in and out of the shadows, trailing smoke balloons behind him.

"What do you know about the paper business?"

"You mean newspapers—or paper manufacturing?"

"Newspapers."

"Not much."

"What papers do you read?"

"*New York Times*, *Wall Street Journal*, *Financial Times*."

He exhaled an enormous mushroom cloud of smoke.

He said, "I like the stories they write about me. What they don't know, they make up."

He grinned like Death itself and added, "With our help, of course."

"You're quite a legend."

He nodded. "Good for business."

He sat down again. "I want you to learn all about the newspaper business. I want you to buy some newspapers for me. Number One isn't involved in this. It's your baby."

"Do you have any particular papers in mind?"

"No. Just want some. Never had any. It might be interesting."

He smiled his Death's-head smile and repeated, "Your baby."

He rose from the chair, extended his moist, bony hand, shook mine, said, "I'll call you in a month or so," and disappeared into the darkness.

Two hours later I was on a plane back to New York.

By the end of the year, Wheeler Enterprises owned three daily newspapers—in Dallas, Kansas City and Seattle. His presence in their industry struck fear into the hearts of journalists. However, as far as I know, he never spoke to anyone at any of the three papers.

Two years later, I sold the three newspapers for him, for a net profit of $27 million—not a fortune to someone who has six or seven billion dollars. I think he was just having some fun.

He liked my work on that project and gave me the lead on others. I rarely saw Number One again. Wheeler gave me my orders directly.

Have I become Number One? I wondered.

I never found out.

Three years after my first meeting with Wheeler, on a pleasant evening in May, I was summoned to his apartment in New York City—a penthouse suite in his own hotel, of course. He seemed quite tense.

He paced and puffed more quickly than usual.

His first words to me were a question: "How old am I, Jason?"

"I'm not sure, Mr. Wheeler. Sixty-something?"

"Sixty-eight," he said.

He was a little older than my estimate.

He asked, "How many times have I been married?"

"Four times."

"Right. Last one died. The other three, I dumped."

He stood in front of me, opened his arms wide and asked, "Do I look like a man in love?"

He didn't, but I decided to take the hint.

"Yes, sir, you do."

He laughed. I had never heard him laugh before. It was not a pleasant sound.

He said, "I met her in Mexico City. At a dinner party I hosted. Her name is Julia Ransom. I intend to marry her."

"That's wonderful. Have you proposed?"

"I have. And she accepted—with one condition."

"One condition?"

He puffed furiously, surrounding himself with a cloak of cigar smoke.

He said, "She is young. Just twenty. When she reaches the age of twenty-five, she will inherit some money. Four hundred million, I think. So she doesn't need my money."

He raised his glowing cigar over his head to emphasize what he was about to say. (He looked like an X-ray of the Statue of Liberty.)

"It is very important for me to marry someone who *doesn't need my money.*"

"Yes, sir. I understand."

"Her mother died when she was a baby. Her father died when she was eleven or twelve. Her half-sister, who is much older, is her guardian. Julia insists that we get her guardian's permission, or she won't marry me."

"Will she have a problem with her inheritance if you don't get permission?"

"No. This is just sentimental nonsense. But I want Julia to be happy."

"Have you spoken to her sister yet?"

There was an ominous silence. I realized what that meant.

After a long pause, Wheeler said, "Jason, I don't negotiate."

I asked, "Where do they live, sir?"

"Southport, Connecticut."

He handed me an envelope and said, "This is all the information you need. You have been invited for the weekend. *This* weekend."

"Yes, sir."

He started to move away from me, then stopped and came back.

He looked intently into my eyes and said softly, "Jason, this is the *big* one. Do not fail me. Need I say more?"

A moment later, only a cloud of cigar smoke marked the spot where he had been.

The Ransom estate in Southport looked down on Long Island Sound from a broad, flat, grassy hill. The caretaker's cottage near the gate was bigger and more luxurious than my parents' home in Long Island.

I had learned a lot about the Ransom sisters—twenty-year-old Julia and thirty-five-year-old Katherine—from the information Wheeler had given me.

When they sojourned in Southport (usually in April, May and June), they lived in a twenty-eight room house with three servants. There were six master bedrooms, seven full bathrooms, a library, a music room, a game room (with two pool tables and two ping pong tables), a ball room, a conservatory, two dining rooms (one seating ten, the other seating forty), a great room (with a two-story cathedral ceiling, a fireplace you could walk into, and an entertainment center that included everything except the Rockettes), indoor and outdoor pools, etc., etc., etc. Not to mention the servants' quarters.

For two people, that's what I call *Lebensraum*.

Julia had left Yale University a few months earlier, in the middle of her sophomore year.

She said (and I quote), "I already know how to be rich, so why bother studying anything else?"

She had a point.

Despite her tender years, she also had a reputation for loving 'em and leaving 'em. Now, at the age of twenty, she had decided to stop all of her gallivanting and settle down with a sixty-eight-year-old eccentric billionaire. Love conquers all!

Julia was the only child of the Second Mrs. Ransom. Katherine was the sole issue of the First, reputed to be a gentle, sensitive woman who married David Ransom when he was still a young haberdasher, starting out in business. By the time his cut-rate clothing chain had sprouted links all over the country ("Buy a King's Wardrobe for a Beggar's Ransom!"), David was a widower, and Katherine was eleven years old. She had artistic ability and eventually graduated from the Rhode Island School of Design. But she was so involved in raising Julia that she never became a professional artist (although she was said to paint "for her own amusement").

Her father left her a trust fund—a slim portfolio of investments, which earned between fifty and sixty thousand dollars a year. His will specified that she could never touch the principal.

Ransom's second wife was apparently as avaricious as he was. She enjoyed "living large," as they say. Like Julia, she also enjoyed playing the field. Rumor had it that she died under mysterious circumstances in Cannes, in the apartment of a seedy French actor who disappeared a few days after her body was discovered.

Wheeler's informants said that Julia thought of her older sister as her mother. She loved her and respected her. That's why I was spending the weekend in Southport.

A pleasant, elderly manservant answered the door, and took my luggage and my car keys. Then he showed me to the conservatory, led me through a potted forest of flowers and ferns, and asked me to be seated at a white, cast-iron table near one of the huge, clear windows that looked out at the Sound. He offered me coffee or tea, and I opted for the former.

He said, "Miss Ransom will be with you in a few minutes."

He returned with a silver coffee pot, cream pitcher, sugar bowl and spoons on a silver tray, as well as cups and saucers and napkins for two, and a plate of muffins. I drained a cup of coffee, munched on a cranberry-nut muffin, watched a tiny sailboat inch across the blue-green water a half-mile away, and wished that I were somewhere else.

A few minutes later, as promised, Miss Ransom—Miss Katherine Ransom—appeared on the scene. I rose. We introduced ourselves and shook hands. Her grip was firm, but not aggressive. Her skin was cool and very smooth.

She was a tall woman, who walked with a vigorous, athletic stride. She was dressed in a white blouse and beige slacks. Her hair was reddish-brown, cut short but not severely. She wasn't pretty, in the conventional sense of the word, but she was attractive. Her dark blue eyes reflected intelligence and confidence. The strong planes of her face and the firm contours of her mouth reinforced that look of self-possession. But when she sat down across the table and looked at me, she seemed to be searching for the right way to begin our conversation.

I stepped into the breach.

"Ms. Ransom," I said, "I realize that this situation is a bit awkward. But I'm sure that, together, we can find a comfortable way through it."

She served herself a cup of coffee, took a sip, and said, "Awkward? A seventy-year-old, certifiably insane, notoriously lecherous hermit, who has divorced three wives and buried a fourth, wants to marry my twenty-year-old sister, and you call that 'awkward'? I might use a stronger term for it. How does 'absolutely disgusting' strike you?"

I felt more relaxed. The negotiation had begun!

I said, "First of all, Mr. Wheeler is only sixty-eight. He is far from insane. He is a very canny businessman. He is also a vegetarian and a teetotaler. His reputation for 'lechery' (as you call it) is as fictitious as the character that tabloid journalists have created—along with the idea that he is a hermit. Mr. Wheeler is very gregarious. In fact, your sister met him at a dinner party he was hosting."

Her eyes hardened a little, but her voice was soft and controlled when she said, "Sixty-eight—seventy—what the hell is the difference? Julia is young enough to be his *descendant*!"

I nodded.

"Ms. Ransom, I agree that there is a significant difference in their ages. But Mr. Wheeler is not your average middle-aged man. He is very active, very strong, and very . . ."

"Old," she interrupted.

"But young enough, attractive enough, to win your sister's heart. Julia accepted his proposal."

Katherine raised her hand, as if she were calling "time out."

She said, "Mr. Greene, I'm not sure I understand *your* role in all of this. Shouldn't Julia's fiancé be here to plead his own case?"

"Mr. Wheeler felt that you could be more objective about your decision if you discussed it with a third party."

"What do you do for a living when you're not a marriage-broker?"

"I'm a lawyer who helps Mr. Wheeler negotiate contracts, things like that."

She smiled. "So he thinks of this as a 'contract'? He must be an incredible romantic."

"No, no, no. He thinks of this as a 'delicate situation,' and he asked me to help him out."

"I assume there'll be a pre-nuptial agreement? Julia's not getting any of his money if and when they divorce, right?"

"Right. It was very important for Mr. Wheeler to find someone who would love him for *himself.*"

Katherine laughed. "If this weren't true, it would be funny."

She sighed, took another sip of coffee and continued. "So, in addition to her youth and beauty, Julia is ideal because she has no need for Wheeler's money. Is that what you're telling me?"

I nodded.

She said, "Doesn't it embarrass you to say these things?"

The late morning sun brushed her hair with crimson highlights and deepened the blue of her eyes.

Despite my better judgment, I answered her honestly.

"No, it doesn't. When I'm negotiating, I'm like an actor. I have a part to play. I create a persona. It isn't always the same. I can be aggressive sometimes, or tentative. Hot or cold. Generous or stingy. It depends on the situation. But I'm not the playwright. I just read the lines."

"And is this a negotiation?"

"Yes, but so is almost everything else we do. If a man asks you for a date, that's really the opening line of a negotiation. He tries to impress you with his offer by demonstrating his charm, his wit, his sophistication. He's negotiating. Even if you're attracted to him, you don't want him to be too sure of himself: you tell him you'll think about it. *You're* negotiating. And if you accept his invitation, you still have to decide when to go out, where you'll go, whether you'll go with other couples. You're negotiating."

Reluctantly, she said, "I suppose that's true. But at least, in your example, the man is asking me for a date with *him*. Not with his boss."

"Ms. Ransom, I'm not asking *you* to marry Mr. Wheeler."

"But I love Julia. She matters to me. She doesn't matter to you. You're just—doing your job."

"Not very well, so far."

She smiled, more warmly than I deserved, and said, "We've only just begun. There are a lot of things I'd like to ask you, but I should give you a chance to refresh yourself after a long drive. Chandler will show you to your room. Why don't we get together for lunch at one o'clock."

"Will Julia be joining us?"

"No, you won't meet her until tomorrow. She's in New York today and she's staying there tonight, visiting a friend of hers—a woman who was a classmate at Yale and *didn't* drop out. But, after all, I'm the one you have to convince."

She smiled again.

"I'll do my best," I said. And I meant it.

Lunch was served on a shady, breezy, screened-in porch.

Katherine had changed into a graceful, sleeveless tunic—a softly-draped, white dress that seemed to barely touch the edges of her body. I thought that she looked even more attractive than she had a few hours ago. The red highlights in her hair burned more brightly in the afternoon sun, and the blue of her eyes reflected the deep, bright colors of the sky and the Sound.

We drank a pleasant white wine, ate grilled salmon and talked.

"Mr. Greene, I realize that this is just an assignment for you, but did you ever wonder why Julia wants to marry Mr. Wheeler? Or aren't you allowed to wonder?"

I dismissed the second question with a smile and said, "I don't know your sister, so I can only guess. You're the expert on Julia. Why did she accept his proposal?"

"I hate to admit it, but I think Julia feels comfortable with your boss. I think they're cut from the same cloth."

"What cloth is that?"

"They're predators. They want. And want. And *want*."

I thought of Wheeler hovering in the damp, smoky shadows of his penthouse steam-bath, reaching out with his bony fingers to buy this and sell that—to wheel and to deal.

I said, "The man has billions of dollars—more than he could spend in a thousand lifetimes. But he'll never have enough. It isn't the spending that matters: it's the *getting*. The hunger for more."

"Julia has that hunger, too. My father was like that. And Julia's mother was even worse."

I took a chance. "And *your* mother: was she the same?"

Katherine studied a cloud for a moment before she answered me.

"No. She was very gentle, very sweet. I can't imagine why she ever married Daddy. And she died before I was old enough to ask her."

"In the years I've worked for Wheeler, I've met a lot of successful people. It doesn't matter what they're successful at—businessmen, artists, writers, actors: they all have that same hunger. They're the hunters—the meat-eaters."

She nodded.

I said, "Ms. Ransom, we seem to agree that your sister and Wheeler are made for each other. Should I assume that my work here is done?"

She was still studying that cloud. It took her a moment to refocus on me.

She shook her head.

"Not at all. I'll grant you that the two of them have a lot in common. But I still think the marriage is a terrible idea."

"Because it's May-December?"

"It's more like 'Death and the Maiden'!"

We laughed.

"And what do *you* want, Ms. Ransom?"

"I want Julia to be happy. And then—I'm going to do some things of my own."

"'Some things'? Like what?"

"Why should I tell you?"

She said that to herself, not to me.

Her eyes studied me the way they had studied that cloud. She was silent, but I could almost hear her setting up a list of "pro's" and "con's." For some reason, the "pro's" won.

She said, "I'm an artist—a painter—not a very good one yet. But I'm going to work at it."

"You don't work at it now?"

She hesitated before she answered, "A little."

For the first time since I had met her, she seemed a little less sure of herself. (Negotiators notice these things. It's our stock in trade.)

"I'd love to see your paintings."

"I don't think that's a good idea."

"Why not?"

"You're just trying to make me more vulnerable. That's your job, isn't it?"

I put out my hand and touched her arm.

I said, "This has nothing to do with my job."

She looked down at my hand on her arm.

She asked, "What *does* it have to do with?"

"I'm not sure."

She said, "Let's have some coffee."

For the next few minutes, we sat quietly and sipped our coffee.

Then she stood up, abruptly, and said, very softly, "Come with me."

I walked behind her, down long corridors and through several high-ceilinged rooms. I didn't notice much of the passing scene; I just watched her, the way she moved, the flow of her white dress.

Her studio was spacious, flooded with sunlight that poured in through huge windows. Several unframed oil paintings were propped against the walls. Two were hanging near the easel, which held a work in progress.

Katherine turned to face me, her back to the easel, as if she were defending it from attack.

"You're still not sure you want me to see your work, are you?"

She hesitated a moment, then stepped aside.

I moved closer. The painting on the easel was a full-length portrait of a slim, blonde, teen-aged girl. She was dressed in jeans and an oversized, man-style shirt. She was sitting on a park bench alone, looking over her shoulder at someone or something beyond the border of the painting. And she was smiling as if she loved that someone or something. Her pose was a subtle blend of childish awkwardness and adult flirtation.

The images were real, but not photographic, shaped by vigorous, bold brushstrokes, deep colors and sharp contrasts of light and shadow.

I said, "Julia."

Katherine smiled.

"How did you know that?"

"It's the way you talk about her. I think you like to remember her when she was still a child—when she was still *your* child."

Katherine nodded. "You're more dangerous than I thought you were," but she smiled again after she said it.

I looked at the two paintings on the wall. One was of a woman wearing a flowered summer dress, standing far away on the bank of a river, silhouetted by the sun behind her, her features unclear.

Katherine said, "That's the way I remember my mother. Always out of reach, out of focus. I wasn't home much when I was growing up. My father sent me away to school, so I would meet the 'right people.' I wish I had known her better."

I pointed to the other painting and said, "Your father."

The man in the painting had apparently just come in from the rain. He was standing in a hallway, unzipping a very wet windbreaker, his hair wet, his shoes leaving trails of water on the floor. He was looking up as if to greet someone. He seemed relaxed and good-humored. And he looked just like Katherine.

I said, "This is like a candid photograph. You seem to have caught him in one split second of time."

"A *rare* split second," she said. "He isn't thinking about his stores, or his money. He isn't frowning and planning and—hunting."

"The two of you have the same face."

"Yes. But, in every other way, I was like my mother. He never forgave me for that. It was as if I had no right to wear his face, as if I had betrayed him. He punished me for it."

"And he rewarded Julia."

Katherine looked into the eyes of her father's image and said, "But he was so busy—opening more stores, making more money—that I had a hand in raising Julia, too."

She added, with pride, "She isn't me, but she isn't *him*, either."

She kept looking into those painted eyes.

After a pause, I said, "Thank you for letting me see your studio. I like your paintings very much."

She turned to me.

"Is that a negotiating technique?"

"No. Your work is very good."

She didn't react to my appraisal.

She said, "Let's have another cup of coffee, and get back to business."

We returned to the screened-in porch. Chandler served more coffee and a plate of assorted scones.

Katherine seemed more at ease now, and more subdued.

"What about you, Mr. Greene? Tell me about yourself. How did you meet your billionaire friend?"

"I was just a middle-class kid from Queens. Went to the state university at Buffalo. I married a girl I met there, then went to Columbia Law School. I set up shop in Manhattan, uptown on the West Side, not far from where we lived. I spent half my time trying to make a living, and the other half on *pro bono* work—taking slumlords to court, defending ghetto kids accused of crimes—that kind of thing."

"You did that?"

"Until my wife divorced me. Until I realized that being poor is no fun for lawyers, either. We both know how nasty rich people can be. But poor people can also be pretty rotten. That's why they go in for robbery, mugging and wife-beating."

"Some rich people beat their wives, too."

"Yes, but they do it for sport."

"Like your Mr. Wheeler?"

"No, that's not one of his faults."

"So how did you meet him?"

"I got my job through the *New York Times*."

"Wanted: Negotiator for Eccentric Billionaire?"

"Not quite."

"How long have you worked for him?"

"About four years."

"Are you earning the salary of your dreams?"

"He's generous. But I never get a chance to spend any money. I'm either traveling, negotiating, or trying to catch up on lost sleep."

"You sound like you need a change."

"So do you."

"Really?"

"Really. Ms. Ransom, picture this: you give your permission, and Julia and Wheeler get married. Of course, you'll see her as often as you can, but she is no longer your responsibility. You're on your own. What would you do?"

"I haven't said that Julia can marry Mr. Wheeler."

"I know. I know. This is just a hypothetical situation. What would you do?"

"I don't know."

"Yes, you do. You've thought about it. You've made your plans."

Katherine started to disagree, but stopped. She shrugged.

Then she said, "Okay. I would find a small house in a quiet, wooded suburban town—either here in Connecticut, or in Westchester—not in New York City, but close enough to get into the City when I wanted to. I would build a studio and work—and work. I might even write children's books and illustrate them. I have some ideas about that."

"That sounds very nice. I wish you could do it."

"You just want to deliver Julia to your boss on a silver platter."

"Ms. Ransom, you should have seen your face when you were talking about your house—your studio—your work. I wish you could do it, for *your* sake."

"Mr. Greene, could we take a break from negotiating for a few hours? There isn't much to do here but we have lots of good books in our library. Or you might like to play some pool."

"As a matter of fact, I brought a lot of paperwork with me that I should do. I can keep busy in my room."

"Fine. Why don't we get together for dinner at seven? In the first-floor dining room. Chandler will show you the way."

"This is hard work, isn't it?"

"Harder than I thought," she said. "I'll see you later."

By six o'clock, I hadn't done any paperwork, but I had made up my mind about what I was going to do. Like an experienced negotiator, I started to plan the best way to approach the subject. Then I stopped planning and decided to just let it happen.

Chandler knocked on my door at ten minutes to seven. I followed him to the first floor dining room—the small one. Katherine was already at the table.

As I sat down, she said, "Julia called. She's staying in town tomorrow, so you won't get a chance to meet her. I'm sorry."

"That's all right. I feel like I already know her."

We had some wine and started dinner with a salad.

I took a deep breath and began. "Ms. Ransom? May I call you Katherine?"

"Yes."

"Then please call me Jason."

"Okay."

"Katherine, I think I've had enough of working for Morton MacNeil Wheeler. Enough of negotiating—of being who I am and what I am."

I took a sip of wine to underline what I had said. Then I continued.

"I want you to let Julia marry Wheeler. From what you tell me about her, she can handle him. They'll have some fun together for a while, but it's not going to last long. Wheeler's marriages never last. She'll get tired of him. He'll start looking for someone else. And that'll be the end of it."

Katherine was surprised.

She said, "Mr. Greene. Jason. Is that what you call 'negotiating'?"

"I'm not negotiating for Wheeler any more. I'm negotiating for myself."

"I don't understand."

"Katherine, I want to start my own law practice again—not a big-time, high-roller practice, but a small-town, one-man law office. I want to be an everyday, ordinary lawyer. I'm going to handle real estate closings, wills, contracts—just the run-of-the-mill things. Maybe teach a course or two. And some *pro bono* stuff, too—enough to keep my conscience happy."

She said, "I still don't . . ."

"I've told you that Wheeler pays me well, and I haven't had much of a chance to spend what I earn. I've made some good investments—enough to give me a cushion, anyway, so I can get through any hard times."

She repeated, "Hard times."

"But none of this matters unless Julia marries Wheeler."

"Why not?"

"Because unless she marries him, you won't be free."

"What have *I* got to do with it?"

"Katherine, you're the most sensible, talented, intelligent, charming woman I've ever met. And you're sort of beautiful, too. Will you marry me?"

She smiled and shook her head. She couldn't decide whether to take me seriously or not.

Finally, she said, "Jason, when the first thing you call a woman is 'sensible,' and the last thing is 'sort of beautiful,' that's not exactly the height of romance."

"Romance doesn't last, Katherine, but *love* can. Say, 'Yes.'"

"We just met today. We don't even know each other."

"I think we *do* know each other. Granted, I'm not very handsome, but I'm in good health and in reasonably good shape. We'll find a modest, charming suburban house and build you a great studio. We'll go to concerts and movies and art exhibits and the theater—eat out a couple of times a week—read the same books—travel now and then. Have a couple of kids.

Once in a while, we'll visit Julia, or meet her in the City, or invite her to stay with us in our modest, charming guest room."

"Jason, I just met you today."

"And I fell in love with you today. Give Julia your permission to marry Wheeler. Then we can get married."

Katherine sat very still, looking at me, for a long time. Then she reached out her hand toward me. I took it in mine. Her skin was very soft and cool.

She said, "I don't do things impulsively."

"I don't, either."

"When would you quit your job?"

"As soon as I tell Wheeler the good news."

"This doesn't make any sense, does it?"

We laughed together.

She said, "You're insane. And I'm insane. Do you prefer Connecticut or Westchester?"

"The real estate taxes are generally lower in Connecticut."

"We could look in Westport or Darien."

"We?"

"We."

I kissed her hand.

I asked, "Yes?"

She said, "Yes."

I said, "You know, Wheeler will never let me come to the wedding."

"It's Julia's wedding, too. She'll insist that you come. And believe me, she'll get her way."

III

OTHER TIMES

FALSE START

September 8, 2012

If I were a younger man, I could be patient. I could wait for our government to finally come to its senses and repeal the laws that were passed just after the turn of the century—laws that forbid us to do the work that we should be doing. But I have been waiting too long.

The promise of my youth—and the possibilities of my middle years, my best years—have disappeared. And still I wait.

We know, in infinite, intricate detail, the shape and structure of the human genome. We have the tools in hand to transform that shape and structure. And still I wait.

We have the power to generate the next stage in our own evolution. We can recreate our own species. And still I wait.

Because of fear. Because of superstition.

"We cannot tamper with Nature," they say.

We do that every day. Do cities and airplanes and computers sprout like flowers in the natural world?

Man has always been the enemy of Nature. He has always struggled to change the world he lives in—to adapt it to his own tastes and desires and needs.

"We will aim for perfection but, in our ignorance, we will create monsters."

The only way to learn is to experiment.

The only way to learn how to recreate ourselves is to experiment on ourselves.

Will there be failures? Of course.

Will there be false starts, dead ends? Of course.

But when we succeed, we will defeat disease and pain and disfigurement—and even death. Perhaps, in order for our species to become immortal, some of us must suffer, some of us must die. Let it be.

I will begin to do what I should have done long ago.

I will find a way.

I will find—someone.

September 19, 2012

His name is Wendell Fairbanks. I saw him in the library a few days ago. I introduced myself, asked him some questions.

He is the perfect choice. He is forty-eight years old. He has no siblings. Both of his parents died in an automobile accident when he was twenty. They left him their house and a small estate that's enough to support him. He doesn't work.

He has serious congenital digestive and respiratory problems that are chronic and disabling. He is a small, homely man, shy and withdrawn. He has no friends. Reading is his sole pleasure, and his taste is eclectic: Jane Austen and *Popular Mechanics;* Zane Grey and the *New Yorker.*

At first, he was suspicious and a little afraid of me. But I was persistent without being aggressive. I pampered him, I soothed him and, at last, I was able to calm his fears. We meet at the library every morning.

September 23, 2012

Yesterday, we went to lunch together at a neighborhood coffee shop. I told him about my work. He has read about genetics in *Scientific American* magazine. He asked some intelligent questions.

I said, "At the moment, we geneticists are in a holding pattern. We can play around with earthworms and fruit flies and cows, but we can't touch the one animal that matters most: *Homo sapiens.* Us."

"Too dangerous, I guess."

"But we can only understand ourselves if we study ourselves. Think of the possibilities. We could reprogram our genes. We could eliminate cancer, heart disease and all of the other defects that weaken us and kill us. And we could make these changes right now—in living human beings."

"Right now?"

"Yes."

He began to cough suddenly—a fierce, racking, gasping cough. It took him several minutes to stop and catch his breath.

I said, "We could free people from illnesses that have plagued them all their lives."

He studied the tabletop for a moment before he asked, "If you experiment on a—person—you could fail, too, couldn't you?"

"Yes."

"That person could die."

"Yes, he could."

"Or he could be cured. He could be—free."

"Free," I said, watching him closely. "For the first time, free."

He said, "Tell me, how would you do these experiments?"

"I would take small samples of the subject's tissue—painlessly, from the soft flesh inside his mouth—extract the genetic material, reshape it, purify it, then reintroduce the improved genes into the subject's body."

"How would that change him?"

"I would use viruses as the carriers—emptied of their own genetic materials—aggressive viruses that attack the nucleus of a cell, destroy the genes in the nucleus and replace them with their own package of genes. I would be infecting my human subject with a better version of himself. The 'disease' would spread, unchecked, and he would be transformed. His infection would cure him."

I could have added, "If it works," but I didn't.

Wendell Fairbanks asked, "How long would this take?"

"A few weeks. A month, at the most."

"You would be breaking the law?"

"Yes. But it's worth the risk."

He repeated just one word: "Risk."

Then he said, "It's worth the risk. Would you be willing to use me as your subject?"

"Are you sure you mean that?"

"Yes. I mean it. I mean it."

My success unnerved me.

I actually said, "Wendell, if things get out of control . . ."

He shook his head and interrupted me: "I want to try."

"You'll have to stay at my place. I have to keep an eye on you twenty-four hours a day."

"The day after tomorrow," he said.

The day after tomorrow, we begin!

September 25, 2012

I set up a makeshift bedroom for Wendell in the storeroom next to my laboratory at home. During the past two years, I've managed to buy all of the equipment I need to duplicate, on a smaller scale, the facilities I have at work.

Wendell brought a pile of books and magazines with him, and made himself at home in his new quarters.

I took tissue samples today. (*Note*: I am maintaining a complete, detailed record of this experiment in my journal. In this diary, I'll be keeping a more personal record.) The GPRO computer program is now analyzing the samples and candling Wendell's genetic material against the templates of "perfect" human genes. When that comparison is finished, I can begin reconfiguring his DNA.

I've set up a closed-circuit television camera that's focused on him, day and night. It is a low-light model that can "see" in the dark. I can watch him from the lab and from my bedroom.

He doesn't sleep much. He reads for hours at night, coughs, cat-naps.

I'm going to change all of that.

September 30, 2012

I used to think that the human genetic code was like an incredibly complicated, microscopic jigsaw puzzle. But when I started working with DNA, I discovered that because this puzzle is alive, when you change one piece, some of the other pieces change, too. Every living being is a unique, complex web of action and reaction—nature and nurture—instinct and will. So the solution also keeps changing.

For some reason, Wendell's genetic code is reacting almost violently to the alterations I'm making in it. I've been reshaping his DNA, purging the errors in it that make him sick. And every time I think I'm finished, I detect a new anomaly—one that wasn't there before. So I go back and reconfigure the new mistake. And then I find another new error.

Or *is* it an error? It doesn't appear in my perfect paradigm so, technically, it's a mistake. But maybe it's an improvement. I don't know.

Wendell doesn't seem to be in a hurry. I've borrowed a whole stack of books for him from the library. He reads. He naps. He doesn't talk much. I guess he's used to being alone.

I've made a decision. I can't wait any longer. Tomorrow, unless my analysis uncovers a known genetic error, I'm going to load up the viruses with the reconfigured DNA and inject it into Wendell's body.

October 1, 2012

I've infected Wendell with his new DNA.

He knows that the changes will come slowly, but he has suddenly become impatient. Every time he coughs, he looks at me as if I've betrayed him.

I've been analyzing a sample of the DNA I injected into him. It keeps changing. Is the same thing happening inside of him?

October 2, 2012

Wendell is still coughing, still reading, still impatient. Still the same.

October 3, 2012

This morning, Wendell seemed calmer. He stayed in bed until after ten, staring out the window at the trees and the sky. He didn't want any breakfast and ate less than usual for lunch and dinner.

I'm writing this in my bedroom. It's nearly midnight. I can see Wendell on the closed-circuit TV picture. He's lying in bed, awake, looking out at the moon and the stars. He isn't coughing.

Today, I again analyzed the sample of DNA I injected into him. It's still changing.

October 4, 2012

Wendell was even quieter than usual today. He ate very little, but drank several glasses of water.

I asked him how he was feeling.

"Fine. A little tired, but fine."

"Aren't you hungry?"

"No."

"Are you sure you're all right?"

"Yes."

"Are you sleeping at night?"

"I'm getting enough sleep."

"Then why are you so tired?"

He didn't answer me. He just smiled benignly, as if he were humoring me.

He hasn't coughed for two days.

The DNA sample is changing more rapidly now.

October 5, 2012

Last night, Wendell didn't sleep at all. But this morning, he seemed more energetic, although he didn't eat any breakfast or lunch.

When I ask him questions now, he usually doesn't answer me. He seems to be thinking about something else, something that demands all of his attention. He sits on his bed for hours, staring at the sky, smiling as if he's listening to a funny story.

I took a tissue sample from him and analyzed the DNA. It was nothing like the template of perfect human DNA.

Now I can only watch and wait

October 8, 2012

I haven't written anything in this diary for a few days because—because there was nothing to write. Wendell stayed in his room. He didn't eat or drink or read. Day and night, he sat in his bed and stared out the window and smiled. He wouldn't answer my questions.

Last night, I sat in the laboratory, watching him on the TV screen. His door, a few feet away from me, was closed.

As I watched, the picture seemed to be blurring. I looked at the screen more closely: the images of the bed, the blanket, the pillow and the window were still in sharp focus. It was only Wendell's image that was blurring. It was as if all the lines that shaped him were melting, as if he were disappearing.

I walked to the door of his room and opened it. My eyes took a moment to adjust to the darkness.

Then I could see him on the bed, staring up at the moon. His skin seemed to be throbbing, pulsing, glowing with an inner light. I was afraid to get too close to him.

Then I heard a faint cracking sound. Slivers of pale yellow light pushed through his skin in hundreds of places, as if he were about to discard his outer layer, shedding it like a worn-out shell. The light grew brighter and brighter until it hurt my eyes.

And then Wendell's body melted away and something new burst out of it—something astonishingly beautiful and strong—something tall and proud and golden-winged—something that had never been born before.

It looked at me and, in its eyes, I saw pride and wisdom and understanding beyond mine or any other human being's. Its thoughts reached into my mind.

It said, "I am the new beginning. I am the first of many. I can create myself."

It turned to the window and somehow, a moment later, it was outside, rising through the night air on the beat of its golden wings, reaching toward the moon and the stars and leaving all of us still clinging to the earth.

It will return someday, I'm sure, with others of its kind. And I'm equally sure that when it does, it will have no need of *us*.

WET

The Peece woke Steven Spector at 6 am. "Spector! Tuesday, September 5. Out of the sack. Train to New York at 7:45. Meeting with Repro.com at 9:30."

Then two minutes of unpleasant, unidentifiable music. Then a repeat of the message. Repeat of music. Repeat of message. Repeat of music.

At 6:15, Steven got out of bed, clicked off the wake-up call and checked the newstream on the Peece screen:

"Prexy Preps Public on Possible Pay Pact. Unions Up Ante"

"Mobster Movie Mayhem Miffs Moms"

"Stocks Sag, Bonds Bomb, IPOs Iffy."

As usual, nothing of interest.

What did I expect? he thought. *Today's weather: sunny and mild?*

He clicked the Peece to a jazz channel, stepped onto his treadmill, walked at 4.3 mph for 30 minutes. Because it was Tuesday, it was a down-day for the Juice in Fairfield, so there was no Air—just necessities: the Peece, the Dryer, the Gym, the Cooker.

As always, it was hot/humid. He was dripping with sweat.

Wet.

He stripped, went into the bathroom, opened the door of the Dryer, closed it behind him and pressed "On."

The Dryer sucked the moisture from the air around him, from his pores, cleaned him, calmed him.

He took a jar of Shave from a shelf on the Dryer wall, rubbed the gel into his face and wiped his beard off with a towel.

When he left the Dryer, he rubbed Breeze all over his naked body. It evaporated slowly, during the next fifteen minutes, cooling his skin as he ate a blueberry muffin and drank orange juice. He sipped iced coffee as he dressed. It was a formal meeting, so he wore a short-sleeved, white shirt, tan slacks, and shoes, not sandals.

At 7:15, he left his bedroom and knocked on the door across the corridor.

"Ready, Marian?" he asked.

Marian Spector, Steven's wife, opened the door to her bedroom. She was tall, long-boned, slim. Her dark hair was cropped very close. Her eyes were gray and opaque. Her mouth was taut.

He hadn't seen her in more than a month.

She asked, "Still a good idea?"

"No commitment," he said. "Just find out: could we, if we wanted to? What are the rules? That's all. Can't do it on-line."

She nodded.

They went to the hall closet and put on their gray slickers and their black rain-boots. He took an umbrella and they left the house.

The damp, shiny streets were almost empty. Long ago, before he was born, most commuting had become telecommuting. Long ago, when it had started to rain everywhere, everytime.

There were explanations: scientists debated, tested, predicted. But explanations don't matter, unless you can change what happened, or prevent it from happening again. They tried; but there was nothing anyone could do about it.

It rained every day, fiercely sometimes, gently sometimes, sometimes mistily. Every day. Everywhere on earth. No one could see the sun or the moon or the stars any more (except on a Peece screen). Sometimes, there was a bright glow behind the clouds.

The seasons blurred into one hot, endless, rainy summer day. Hot/humid winds. Hot rains.

Springsummerfallwinterspringsummerfallwinter.

People moved indoors. They rarely traveled. They vacationed electronically—on the Net. They studied, worked, shopped, visited, entertained themselves—on-line. Manufacturing, farming, transportation were robotized—monitored and controlled on-line. Almost everyone, almost everywhere, rich or poor, had at least one Peece (free, if you couldn't afford it) and access to the Net (free, if you couldn't afford it).

To run it all, to maintain it all, Governments took a flat, no-loopholes, 30% bite out of personal and corporate incomes. (Some governments took more.)

Another 10% went to Protex.com—the Hackers' clan that guaranteed Internet security. (In some places, Protex.com took more.)

We had created a virtual world just in time to take the place of the real one.

The umbrella couldn't keep them dry. As they walked toward the railroad station, an aggressive, hot, irritating wind stirred up the heavy raindrops and sprayed their faces. In the thick, humid air, they began to sweat; it felt as if the rainwater was splashing against their bodies, even through the slickers.

Wet.

They didn't speak to each other.

The Fairfield station was a decaying memory of another time. A handful of passengers waited with them for the first morning train to New York City. (The New Haven Railroad schedule was simple: two trains in the morning, two at night.)

A shabby steel fossil, five cars long, edged up to the platform and shuddered to a stop. They boarded it cautiously, as if it were a gateway to the past.

But this was a gateway run without engineers or conductors or ticket agents. It was simple stuff for self-monitoring, self-repairing supercomputers, whispering binary messages to the rolling stock. Tickets were bought and charged on the Net, printed out, checked by sensors. No people required. Just 1s and 0s, bits and bytes.

Steven and Marian sat in aisle seats across from each other: neither of them wanted to sit near a window and watch the raindrops shatter against the glass and streak it with water.

Wet.

As they walked from Grand Central Station to the Repro.com office on Madison Avenue, the hot wind pushed ebony clouds across the gray sky and swirled viciously between the dark, half-empty buildings. The rain assaulted Steven and Marian from every direction. He fought to hold onto the umbrella.

Repro.com was on the sixth floor of a narrow, twenty-story, black-glass tower. They had never been there before.

The reception area was a gray, bare-walled room divided into a dozen cubicles, separated by low, gray partitions. Each cubicle contained two chairs, a table, and a Peece. Three other couples were already working at the Peeces in their cubicles.

When Steven and Marian entered the reception area, a disembodied female voice said, "Cubicle number four, please," and the Peece screen in one of the vacant cubicles began to flash the number "4."

The dense carpet clung to their feet as they walked, as if it were trying to discourage them.

When they sat down in Cubicle 4, the Peece asked them a series of questions: Name? Address? Age? Occupation? Income? Race? Religion? State of health? Date of marriage? Children?

He keyed in all of the answers for both of them until he came to the last item: "ReproReason?"

Reason?

They looked at each other, dully. They had never discussed a "reason." Did they have a reason? She had said, "We're thirty. It's time for a child."

Was that a reason?

Marian stared at him opaquely, helplessly, and mouthed the word "reason" without actually saying it, as if it were obscene.

"ReproReason?"

Steven whispered, "Parental instinct?"

She shrugged, nodded.

He keyed it in.

"Parental instinct" looked ridiculous on screen, but the Peece accepted it.

Why do we want a child? he thought. *Do we still love each other? We hardly know each other any more. And we'll never get to know the child.*

The Peece screen assigned a room to each of them for the fertility/genetics test.

Steven's test required a sample of his semen. A large-screen Peece (with HeadSet) offered him a selection of Fantasex. He was tense, almost angry: the Fantasex he chose was cruel. When he came, he felt the tension and the anger dissipate.

The Peece said that they would receive their results on-line in two days.

Steven met Marian in a small waiting room beyond the testing area.

As she approached him, he was reminded of how beautiful she had been. Slim, dark-haired, gray-eyed. He had met her at a social when they were twenty years old. She was so slender and awkward, with barely discernible breasts and narrow hips, that she had almost seemed like a very pretty boy. But when he danced with her, he felt the soft, warm shell of flesh on her hips. The gentle pressure of her fingers on his shoulder was a soft chain that held him close to her. In the humid warmth of the dance floor, her breath was somehow cool and sweet. And the grayness of her eyes glowed with a heat that he had never felt before.

Now there was no glow.

Now he couldn't see past her eyes.

Now they were thinking about having a baby.

She said, "Home," in a tone that was both question and answer.

When they left the building, the rain had almost stopped, but not quite. Steven looked up and down Madison Avenue. There were a few people in the street, wrapped in gray slickers, black-booted, huddled under umbrellas.

He said, "I feel like staying in town. Do you?"

"No."

"You take the umbrella," he said.

Before she left him, Marian hesitated for a moment. She watched him as if she expected something to happen. The taut line of her mouth softened, and her eyes became almost transparent.

She turned and walked away.

Steven went in the opposite direction, north on Madison Avenue. The rain was only a mist. Invisible drops coated his hair and dampened his face. His feet splashed through murky puddles.

Wet.

He turned west on 63rd Street. The other gray-slickered pedestrians ignored him, keeping their umbrellas lowered, watching the wet sidewalk. He wondered why they were in New York City.

At the corner of Fifth Avenue, he heard sounds that seemed out of place: music, laughter, shouting. He followed the sounds to a storefront between 64th and 65th Streets.

It was a restaurant. The double doors were wide open. On a stage at the far end of the long, narrow room was a trio of singers. Two of them were playing guitars; one was playing a banjo. A dozen ceiling fans spun noisily overhead. There were twenty or thirty tables scattered around the place, and every chair at every table seemed to be occupied. People stood along the walls, or at the bar, holding drinks or plates of food. Waiters, carrying heavily-loaded trays, dashed in and out of the kitchen, dodging each other at a reckless, almost slapstick velocity. Everyone was talking, singing, shouting, laughing.

Since the days when he had attended socials, Steven had never seen so many people together in one place. But never in his life had he seen people like *these*.

They were a crazyquilt of colors and styles. The women wore bright flowered dresses, or long, flowing pastel robes, or short black leather skirts, or baggy silk pants, or sweat suits, or shorts. The men's wardrobe was just as bizarre, just as varied, just as colorful, and many of them had beards and moustaches. Some (women and men) wore hats, caps, bandanas, earrings, necklaces, amulets, tiaras, bracelets. Some didn't. Some had long hair, some had short hair, some (men *and* women) had shaved heads.

What was even more remarkable to Steven was that so many people could endure so much *contact*—could be so close together, touching each other, side by side, face to face, in that storm of noise and confusion.

Looking at that chaotic crowd, he found himself gasping for air: he opened his mouth wider to suck more air into his lungs.

He turned to escape and almost collided with a young woman who was headed in the opposite direction.

He said, "Sorry," and tried to pass her, but she moved to block him.

She said, in a hard-edged, but pleasant voice, "Not so fast, my good man. We meet, as if by chance, but who among us can say that it was not Fate—Kismet?—that brought us together."

She was obviously one of them. She was short and plump. Her long blond hair (which was wet) was streaked with blue and green, and tied back with a red ribbon. She wore purple eye-shadow and bright red lipstick. Huge, gold hoop earrings pierced her lobes, accompanied by rows of diamond studs in the shell of each ear. She wore black, skin-tight jeans and a black sweater, with a multicolored scarf tied around her neck and a matching cape over her shoulders.

He said, "Going home."

She blocked his path again.

She said, "Not yet, my gray and gloomy friend. For I am not done with thee."

He started to speak, but didn't know what to say.

She raised her hand, touched his shoulder and asked, "What drives thee home? A rendezvous with thy true love? I think not. What then? Got the hots to get on-line?"

She laughed and patted his shoulder and added, "There, there, my dear. Be not offended."

She stepped back, surveyed him head to foot to head, and said, "Allow me to introduce myself. I am Winifred Boyle, scholar, poet, musician, performance artist, *lover*. But you can call me Guinevere."

"Guinevere?"

She said:

"Leodogran, the King of Cameliard,
"Had one fair daughter and none other child.
"And she was fairest of all flesh on earth.
"Guinevere, and in her his one delight."

She swept her right hand across her body and bowed low to him.

She said, "You don't know what the hell I'm talking about, do you?"

"I'm . . . Going home."

But she was in his way again.

She said, "I would love to get you to say more than those little monosyllabic, computerized grunts. You know, there's a story about George

Bernard Shaw—he was a famous playwright two hundred years ago—a great playwright—but he was like you: he didn't enjoy talking to people. One day, at a party, a young girl came over to him and said, 'I just bet my friend that I could get you to say three words.' And Shaw said, 'You lose.'"

She laughed. Steven just stared at her.

She asked, "What's your name, sweetheart?"

He answered automatically, "Steven Spector."

She laughed. "I lose!" Then she added, "Steven, would you join me for a light repast? I know that this place seems awfully crowded but, as luck would have it, I am the daughter of the proprietor, and I can get us the perfect table, right by the bandstand—just by snapping my fingers."

She snapped her fingers, as if to prove that she could do it.

She continued, "And the food and drinks are on me—not literally, of course." Then, eyes narrowed, she added, "Unless you prefer it that way! Come, my darling: come in and taste the rainbow."

She put her arm through his, turned him around and led him into the restaurant.

She was greeted with shouts and cheers. "All hail Guinevere! Tis the Queen herself! Your Majesty!"

A dark, bearded man shouted, "That turkey on your arm doesn't look like the King, or Lancelot. He looks too *Dry*!"

Laughter on all sides.

She said, "Nay, nay. Perhaps his outer shell be Dry. But if ye look into his heart and soul, he is as pure—and *Wet*— as the driven snow. My friends, my boon companions, feast your eyes upon Sir Galahad! And ladies, he hath promised to show me his Holy Grail!"

More laughter.

She found the perfect table by the bandstand, waved the occupants away and sat down with Steven.

She asked, "What wouldst thou drink, my sweet Galahad? Wine, beer, booze, soda, juice, milk. Name it, my dear, and it is thine."

Although the restaurant was crowded, it was surprisingly cool: the noisy ceiling fans kept the air moving. But Steven felt trapped in a forest of bodies and faces and voices and music and colors. Everything seemed to close in on him.

He said, "Beer."

"Wouldst thou also like a snackeroo? Sandwich? Salad? Stew?"

"Just beer."

She passed the word to a waiter dodging by. "Sam: one beer. And the usual for me."

She put her hand on his and said, softly, "Steven, try to relax. These are my friends. We're just having fun."

She smiled at him and, for the first time, he realized how young she was: nineteen or twenty. And, behind all of that glitter, she was almost pretty.

The waiter brought him a tall stein of beer and gave Guinevere a Manhattan.

She raised her glass and toasted him. "Cheers—and cheer up!"

He repeated, "Cheers," and drank several mouthfuls of beer. It was deliciously cold and bittersweet.

The trio began to sing a song about a train—"called the City of New Orleans"—and everyone (except Steven) joined them. They sang three more songs that everyone (except Steven) knew. Then the banjo player said that they were "taking a break," and the trio left the bandstand.

By this time, Steven had finished his beer and ordered a second one.

Guinevere asked, "Where are you from, Galahad?"

"Fairfield, Connecticut."

"What do you do for a living?"

"Accountant."

"Would you do me a favor? Would you stop talking like fucking email? See if you can put together a whole sentence. Say, 'I am an accountant, Guinevere.' Come on, try it. Repeat after me: 'I am an Accountant. I am a number-cruncher. I am an asset to my friends, and a liability to my enemies.'"

She laughed. He smiled.

He said, "I am an accountant—Guinevere."

She raised her eyes to the Heavens and shouted, "Halleluyah! Now hear the word of the Lord! Galahad has spoken an entire, honesttoGod sentence. He even smiled at me!"

She leaned across the table and kissed Steven on the lips, lightly—a friend's kiss.

She said, "Does this place—all these people—really scare you? Or is it just me?"

"I—we don't do this kind of thing."

"I know. Most people don't."

"It's hard for me. I have friends. Colleagues. On-line. Not in the same room."

"What about your family?"

"I have a wife."

"No, I mean your *parents, sisters, brothers*."

"I know their names. I know what they look like. We've been in contact occasionally."

She touched his face with her hand, stroked his cheek. There were tears in her eyes. She didn't say anything.

He paused, then said, "We—my wife Marian and I—were in New York City today about having a baby."

Guinevere ignored what he thought was an important piece of information and said, "Galahad, my apartment is a couple of blocks from here. Come with me there. It's quiet. I have beer in the refrigerator. Come and talk to me. Will you?"

He shrugged, hesitated, then said, "Yes."

Her apartment was a huge studio on the top floor of a gray, ten-story concrete building. The shades were drawn. Two ceiling fans spun overhead, and a huge window fan drew the damp air out of the room. It was fairly cool.

The décor was just like her: eclectic, garish, friendly.

When she handed him a glass of beer, she said, "Are you more comfortable here, away from the people and the noise?"

He nodded and asked, "Do you live here alone?"

"Yes."

"Where is your Peece?"

"I don't have one." She frowned. "And, Jesus, it isn't a 'Peece.' I hate that word. I don't have a *Personal Computer*—a *PC*."

"How do you go on-line?"

"I don't. Not here, anyway. At work, I do."

"What work?"

"I'm a designer. I do layouts for magazines and newsletters."

"On-line?"

"Unfortunately, yes. But I also design books. *Real* books. A few people still buy them."

"I read books."

"No, no, Galahad. I don't mean pixels on a screen. Or print-outs. I mean books that you hold in your hand."

She crossed the room, pulled two books from a shelf on the wall, returned to him and put them in his lap. He picked one up.

She said, "Open it."

He did.

She said, "Read the title out loud."

"*The Complete Short Stories of Edgar Allan Poe*. I've read Poe."

She said, "Turn the pages. Look at the shapes and sizes of the letters, the way the page numbers are designed, the marbled edges of the paper. Feel the weight of it. That's a book."

"Did you design it?"

"No. I wish I had." She picked up another book from his lap, a small, slim volume with a leather cover. "This one is mine."

He opened it and read, "*As I Pondered in Silence: Selected Poems of Walt Whitman*."

As he turned the pages, he said, "I like the way the paper looks and feels. And I like the little pictures."

"Whitman said, 'I celebrate myself.' Do you celebrate yourself, Steven?"

She didn't call me Galahad, he thought.

He said, "Don't know what that means."

"Are you happy to be who you are?"

"Should be. Lately, I'm not sure."

"Why not?"

"Don't know. Uneasy."

"Jesus Christ, Steven, you're talking like a machine again! Say, 'I don't know.'"

"Sorry," he said, then corrected himself: "I'm sorry. Recently, I sometimes get angry, but I don't know why."

"Did you talk to your wife about it?"

"No."

"Why not?"

"She has *her* life and I have mine. She has *her* work and I have mine. She has *her* friends and I have mine."

"Don't you talk at breakfast? At dinner?"

"We don't eat together. Our schedules are different."

"When do you see her?"

"If I have something to tell her, I send her an email."

"Don't you live in the same house?"

"Yes. But she has *her* space, and I have mine."

"You don't sleep together?"

"No."

"What about sex?"

"There are already too many people in the world. Fantasex is better than real sex: more variety, more partners, but no babies."

"Sounds great! Getting head from a HeadSet. Did you ever make love to each other?"

"In the beginning."

"Did you like it?"

"Yes. But Fantasex is better. There are no limits, no pressures. We can do anything we like, without worrying."

"And if you want to have a baby, that's a lab job, right?"

"So we can be sure that the baby is healthy."

"And when do the proud parents get to see this healthy baby? Once a year?"

"Whenever we want to."

"But the Caregivers bring up the kids, right?"

"They're trained for that."

"Do you know who brought me up? My mother and father. Crazy, huh? And that's not all! They made me by making love! Can you believe it?"

He stood up.

He said, "Now you're angry. I'm going home."

She said, "You hate the rain, don't you, Steven? You hide from it. Your whole goddamn world hides from it. We don't hide from it. We walk in the rain. We open our mouths and drink it. We clean ourselves in showers of water. We even call ourselves *Wets*. And we're proud of that because, to us, wet means 'free.' It means we're not hooked up to that goddamn Net every minute of every day. It means that we make love to *people*. It means that we live in *families*.

"Steven, it isn't raining all the time because some vengeful God is pissed off at us. It's raining because of something *we* did—something that screwed up the air and the clouds. And if we did it, we've got to *live* with it, not run away from it. We can't spend our lives trying to stay Dry. We've got to get *wet*."

He put on his slicker and his boots.

"Goodbye, Winifred."

"Goodbye, Steven."

At home that evening, he searched on-line for information about the "*Wets*." He was surprised at how much there was. In a sociology textbook, he read:

The Wets. Contemporary sub-culture of American/Western European society, consisting of approximately 40,000 individuals clustered in highly interactive, urban enclaves (in such cities as New York, San Francisco, Paris, London, Prague, Florence). The Wets are *atavistic*: they take pleasure in reviving inefficient, obsolete practices, e.g., engaging in direct sexual reproduction, raising their own children, living in extended family groups. They use the Net as infrequently as they can, preferring personal interaction. Although most governments officially disapprove of their behavior, the Wets are tolerated because they provide a variety of valuable services to the economy. Among the Wets are many highly skilled scientists, engineers, programmers, artists, writers, entertainers, inventors. Our political leaders agree that the Wets' contributions to society outweigh the group's negative, but minimal, influence on normal citizens, or *Drys*, as they call us.

As he dug deeper, exploring Wets' sites, as well as Drys', Steven began to understand how the Wets had affected his own life, even though they lived on the edges of society. In science, technology, the arts, they had shaped much of the modern world. Because they weren't in the mainstream, there was no official acknowledgement of their contributions. But, for more than fifty years, they had been well paid for their services, and they had been allowed to live the way they chose—i.e., *atavistically*.

Steven's childhood was a typical Dry childhood. He had been raised by Caregivers in a quiet, suburban setting. The City—any city—had little appeal for him. As a child, he played and swam at local parks and beaches. As a teenager, his AgeGroup's activities included team sports and dancing at the occasional Socials. But his education was solitary: his Peece was his teacher and, usually, his companion: it played music for him, it read to him, it played chess with him, it taught him about sex and, sometimes, it led him to anonymous places where he could explore his darker self.

And all the while, there was another kind of world out there, another kind of people.

I've lived every day of my life in ignorance, Steven thought. *Just beneath the surface, just around the corner, is another society—intelligent, inventive, artistic—and completely invisible. Is it the only one I've missed?*

He remembered the restaurant, a Bedlam of noise and shapes and sounds and voices. Even in memory, its images frightened him—the closeness, the intimacy, the raw edges. There were no barriers, no protection.

And no umbrellas.

He crossed the corridor and knocked on Marian's door. He had to knock again before she heard him.

She looked very tired.

She asked, "Where'd you go today?"

"Restaurant."

"Why?"

He shrugged and said, "I'd like to have supper with you. Tonight."

"Why?"

"You're my wife."

She said, "Tomorrow, maybe."

She began to close the door. He blocked it with his arm, then reached in and touched her face with his fingertips. She looked down at his hand, as if it were a stranger.

He said, "Tomorrow, maybe," and she closed the door.

Two days later, they received an e-mail from Repro.com:

"Re: Steven & Marian Spector

"Fertility: 9+ (1 Lowest, 10 Highest)

"DNA: 8+ (1 Lowest, 10 Highest)

"ReproPermit: Granted."

Steven emailed Marian: "Congrats. Dinner together at 7 tonight?"

She responded: "Okay."

At 7, they met in their ComRoom—their Common Room—neutral ground where they could spend time together, or entertain guests. There was a couch, two chairs, a dining room table for four and a Cooker in the corner.

Steven opened the Venetian blinds on the window that looked out at the woods behind the apartment complex. The rain rattled on the glass. The moon glowed weakly behind the clouds.

It was an up-day for the Juice, so the Air was on full force, cooling the apartment.

He prepared dinner: Caesar Salad, Veal Marsala. They finished with her favorite dessert—pecan pie—and coffee. He had selected a Merlot to accompany the meal.

Marian was very quiet. She ate and drank mechanically, without apparent pleasure. She looked out the window, or at her food, but not at Steven.

Finally, when they were finishing their coffee, he asked, "You want a baby, don't you?"

"Not sure."

"Wasn't that why we went to Repro.com?"

"Not sure."

"What aren't you sure about?"

She looked at him and said, "Everything," flatly, without expression, but he could see the fear in her eyes.

He said, "Marian, remember the first time we met? Do you?"

She said, "Yes," without warmth.

"You were the only girl I wanted to dance with, the only girl I wanted to be with."

Her eyes softened: she was beginning to actually think about that night.

She asked, "Why?"

"You were beautiful. Graceful. Sure of yourself."

She repeated, "Sure of yourself," in a tone that mocked the words.

"I never see you any more."

"Busy."

"I want to see you more."

"Why?"

"Don't we still love each other?"

She didn't answer him.

He stood up, came around the table and reached for her. She stood up and let him embrace her, but she didn't respond. He kissed her hair, stroked it, held her against him. She rested her hands on his chest, passively.

He said, "I want us to spend time together again, to talk again. Please, Marian. I want to find out if we still love each other."

For a long minute, she didn't answer him.

Then she said, "Okay."

"Saturday, I want you to go into the City with me."

"The City?"

"Yes. There are things to see. People to see."

"Okay."

The rain splashed against the window. The ghost of the moon glowed in the clouds.

She rested her head on his shoulder and sighed.

In New York City, the Saturday morning rain was virtually windless. The large, clear drops pelted the umbrella but, otherwise, kept their distance. The clouds seemed whiter than usual.

Steven and Marian walked uptown on Fifth Avenue from 43rd Street.

The streets were almost empty.

On the corner of 54th, a huge sign hung on a flagpole over the entrance to a store: "FLEA MARKET! BARGAINS GALORE! MAKE YOUR BEST OFFER!"

He said, "Let's see what kind of bargains they have."

"Don't need anything."

"Just looking."

The interior of the store was a single, very large, high-ceilinged room filled with dozens of tables. From table to table, the merchandise varied: jewelry, gourmet delicacies, books, clothing, paintings and sculptures, hats, scarves, belts, shoes, antique appliances, obsolete Peeces. Handwritten cardboard signs touted the goods and the cut-rate prices, but there was also a steady stream of promotional chatter from the merchants— all of whom were Wets. The customers were a mixed bag of Wets and a few Drys.

Marian said, "Odd-looking people here."

"Call themselves 'Wets.' I met some the last time we were in the City."

"Wets?"

"Looked them up on the Net. Fringe group in some big cities. Don't live the way we do. Live the way people used to, a hundred years ago."

"Why?"

"They want to."

"We *let* them?"

"Yes. They're engineers, scientists, artists. Very creative. Very productive. We use what they produce. How they live is up to them."

"Never knew about them."

"Had no reason to know. They call us Drys. Not a compliment."

She studied the Wets more closely, with more interest.

They walked past a table loaded with colorful scarves. He picked one up and asked her, "Like this?"

"Don't know."

He held it up alongside her face.

He said, "These colors match yours. I want to buy it for you."

"Don't need it."

"I want you to have it."

He asked the Wet behind the table, "How much?"

"Eight dollars, *mon ami*."

"Can I charge it on-line?"

"Is the Pope a Catholic?"

The question seemed irrelevant, but Steven answered it anyway. "Of course he is." (Maybe it's some kind of Wet ritual, he thought.) Then he repeated, "Can I charge the scarf on-line?"

The Wet stared at him for a moment, stroked his thick, blonde beard, muttered, "*Mon Dieu!*" and produced a laptop. "Just key in your ID and the amount."

As Steven completed the transaction, the Wet wrapped the scarf in waterproof paper and handed it to Marian.

"Don't need it," she said.

The Wet said, "Wear it in good health."

When they left the Flea Market, they continued north on Fifth Avenue, browsing in a couple of Wet-run art galleries near 59th Street and a second-hand clothing store (with a Wet proprietor) called RetroFit. Steven almost bought a tan coat—the Wet called it a "raincoat"—but he thought it was too expensive.

He said, "Let me try it on again."

He looked at himself in the full-length mirror. All of his life, he had worn a gray slicker. So had everyone else he knew—all the Drys. The raincoat made him look different. It made him feel different, too. All he needed was a beard, or a bandana, and he would look like a Wet.

Marian said, "I like that. You look handsome."

Then she blushed, like a thirty-year-old teenager.

He said, "I'll buy it. And wear it right now. But only if you wear your scarf."

"Okay."

He asked the clerk to wrap his slicker. He put on the raincoat. Then he unwrapped Marian's scarf and tried to figure out how to drape it around her neck. It wasn't easy.

A hard-edged, pleasant voice said, "I'm sorry, Steven, you haven't got a clue. Let me assist you in this surprisingly romantic endeavor."

Winifred Boyle appeared from behind a rack of garish clothing, which her own garments easily outgarished.

She took the scarf from Steven and, with a magical flourish, draped it beautifully around Marian's neck.

Marian looked back and forth from Steven to Winifred and back again, as if she were watching a tennis match.

Steven said, "Marian, this is Winifred Boyle. We met last week. Winifred, this is my wife, Marian."

Winifred shook Marian's hand vigorously, dramatically, and gushed, "*Enchanté!* My dear Marian, my *deardear* Marian, I can't tell you how delighted I am to finally meet you in the flesh! You are all that Steven said you were—and, if I may be so bold, much, much more!"

Marian responded to this avalanche of words with a polite bow of her head, and then she smiled sweetly. (Steven couldn't remember the last time she had done that.) She was so beautiful. Smiling. Almost relaxed. The bright colors of the scarf were reflected like tiny rainbows in her gray eyes.

Winifred asked, "Have you made any definite plans for lunch? No? Then please allow me to propose a delicious, inexpensive nosh at a marvelous coffee shop on Lexington Avenue where, as it happens, a bosom buddy of mine—an exceptionally talented composer and pianist—is performing some of her new work today."

Marian said, "Sounds nice."

In the street, Winifred walked between them, one arm linked in Steven's, one in Marian's. Steven tried, with moderate success, to hold the umbrella over the two women. Fortunately, the rain had dwindled to a light drizzle.

Winifred said, "Marian: Steven told me that he is an accountant. What, pray tell, do you do to make a buck?"

"Statistician. Develop and analyze marketing surveys, opinion surveys."

"So you, too, like your husband, are a cruncher of numbers. Could anyone doubt the compatibility of such a pair?"

Marian asked, "Your profession?"

"I am a designer of books—a purveyor of shapes and colors and forms—a packager of prose and poetry. Of course, I have dabbled in other arts, as creator and performer: the Drama, the Opera, the Ballet."

Marian was skeptical: "So young. So many things?"

Winifred laughed and said, "I've tried *everything*. Why not? How else can you discover what you do well?"

The coffee shop, as Steven expected, was crowded and noisy. He put his arm around Marian's shoulder to shield her; she leaned against him. A tall, red-haired, middle-aged woman in a long, pastel robe waved Winifred over to a table near the front of the shop.

The woman kissed Winifred's cheek and said, "I saved this spot for you, dear," and added, politely, "and for your friends."

Winifred said, "Eleanor Graham, meet Steven and Marian Spector."

Eleanor shook hands with each of them and said, "I'm going on in a few minutes. I'll see you later."

She disappeared into the crowd.

They ordered lunch.

A few minutes later, just after the food and drink had arrived, Eleanor reappeared, sat down at the grand piano, acknowledged the applause of the crowd, and said, "Thank you, friends. This will be the first public performance of five new etudes and my sonata in F major."

She took a long, deep breath, and began to play.

The coffee shop was suddenly silent.

Eleanor's music was muscular, jagged, unapologetic. As she played, she sometimes hummed along with the music, as if she were singing a wordless aria. Her voice wasn't a distraction: it added to the intensity of the performance.

The sound of live music was not as clear and pure as the carefully edited, digitally perfect music Steven heard on the Peece. And there was background noise from the street and from the audience in the coffee shop. But he could feel the vibrations of it—the overtones, the dynamics—in a different way: as if his body had become a sounding board.

Marian reached for his hand and grasped it tightly. They looked at each other. She pressed his fingers even harder, then relaxed them and looked back at Eleanor.

After the performance, and several rounds of applause and cheers, Eleanor joined them at the table.

Winifred kissed her enthusiastically and praised her extravagantly.

Marian said, "Wonderful. Really wonderful. Thank you."

Eleanor kissed her.

Steven said, "That was beautiful."

Eleanor kissed him, said, "I'm hungry," and ordered a Hamburger Deluxe and a bottle of wine.

Eleanor said to Marian, "I haven't seen you and your husband before, have I? You don't come in to the City much, I guess."

"Almost never."

Winifred said, with comic gravity, "What you see before you, Eleanor, is a Dry couple that is beginning to get Wet."

Steven smiled.

Winifred continued, "Even that smile is something new for him. Please note that he bought a raincoat today and now wears it in place of his goddamngray slicker. And, what is more, he purchased a colorful scarf for his lady love—that scarf—which now adorns her throat. I ask you, are these the actions of a Dry?"

Eleanor shook her head.

Winifred said, "I've got a feeling in my bones that I've got me two new recruits."

Steven said, "Recruits?"

"I assure you, my dear, I used that word advisedly. Do you think that I latched onto you simply by accident? No, no, my benighted friend. Ditch all that Kismet crap. I seized upon you in order to save your ass and, hopefully, the rest of you, as well. And now, your beloved Marian has been added to my agenda."

Marian said, "What agenda?"

"To free both of you. From your dry Dry world."

Marian said, "We *are* free."

Winifred patted her cheek, as if she were a child, and answered, "No, you're not. But you *can* be."

She took a sip of wine, leaned back in her chair and said, "Years ago, my father explained it all to me. He said that it wasn't the endless fucking rain that drove everyone inside—that locked them into the Net—and kept them alone and isolated, watching the world through the screens of their PCs. He said that the rain was only an excuse.

"Long before the rains came, people were becoming more and more interested in themselves and less interested in everyone else. They stopped caring about their neighborhoods, or their families, or the needs of other people. And the new technologies made it ohsomuch easier to feel that way.

"As the Net grew and spread its wings, everything became available on it. You could work at home, see the latest movies, listen to any kind of music, read any book or magazine you wanted to read, travel anywhere in the world, enjoy the most dangerous adventures or the weirdest sex without any risk.

"And of course, when you were on the Net, you could be anybody you wanted to be. You were who you *said* you were: prettier, younger, sexier, wealthier—you name it. In a chat room, your opinion always mattered. In FantaSex, you were always hot stuff.

"So, as the Net spread, it pushed people further and further apart—but only because they wanted it to."

She took another sip of wine and continued: "Marriage was still okay: it was a comforting holdover from the past. It made people feel as if things hadn't changed that much. It also gave them a taste of real sex. And of course, we still needed to have kids, or we'd become extinct. But families had become too much of a hassle. So they came up with the Overpopulation

Shtick: there are too many people in the world, so we have to regulate how many babies are born. And we have to make sure that every one of them is perfect. Enter Repro.com!"

Eleanor applauded politely.

Winifred acknowledged the applause with a bow of her head and continued: "You send your eggs and sperm to a lab, and they take it from there. And you don't have to be bothered bringing up your offspring. Caregivers do that for you. You know who your kids are, and they know their parents. You see each other once in a while. But it's the Caregivers who are really their Mamas and Papas—and then the PCs take over. Boom! Another Dry-as-dust generation has been created. There is Peece on earth!"

Winifred paused for a moment, then raised an index finger and said, "But one thing didn't compute: the Dry life doesn't produce creativity. It doesn't produce inventors— artists— innovators. Creative thinking doesn't grow in isolation. It only happens when people talk to each other, argue, bounce ideas off each other. Enter the Wets!"

Eleanor applauded again.

"The Wets were creative. They had the talents that Dry life never produces. And they knew that they had to be part of a community, so that others could teach them and challenge them. The Dry world needed them. So it let them live outside—in the rain—in families—in communities—in the real world. And the Wets are what keeps everything going—the Net, the trains, the Arts, the Sciences. Without us, the Dry world would dry up."

She smiled at her turn of phrase.

She continued: "I don't know how many of us there are. No one does. But there are more of us every day. Because we keep recruiting. Which is what I'm doing right now. Steven. Marian. Come join the party. Get Wet!"

Marian said, "Our jobs. Our careers."

Winifred said, "No sweat. You can do just what you're doing today. Right on the Net. But you don't have to *live* on the Net. You and Steven can live together, with a whole bunch of people around you— weirdos like me and Eleanor. You can have fun together. You can have sex together. You can make babies and bring them up together."

Steven said, "We wouldn't be very good at living that way."

"Not to worry. We'll teach you, sweetheart. Maybe someday, if you're lucky, you two could have a brilliant, gorgeous kid like me!"

Marian smiled and said, "My God!"

They laughed.

Steven said to Winifred, "We've got to talk about this. We have to think about this."

Marian added, "Together."

Winifred said, "Go, my friends. Talk and think. And be not afraid. Perhaps there are more Wet things in Heaven and earth than are dreamed of in your philosophy. But we can teach you to dream."

When Steven and Marian left the coffee shop, it was raining hard again and a gusty wind was blowing. He opened the umbrella. They walked through the shiny streets, her arm locked tightly in his.

Steven said, "I wouldn't even think about what she said, except for the way I feel lately. Always angry."

Marian said, "Always afraid."

"We used to live together, when we first got married. We used to eat together. Make love. We could do it again."

She repeated the sentence softly. "We could do it again."

"It wouldn't be easy to change everything."

"No. Wouldn't be easy."

"You get used to doing what you want, when you want to do it."

"Live your own life."

They walked silently for a few minutes. There was a park ahead of them. They walked into it, down a winding path. It was early Autumn and, despite the heat, the trees continued to respond to ancient, seasonal patterns: some of them had begun to lose their leaves.

Steven said, "Do you want to try it, anyway?"

"Don't know."

As they moved past a thick stand of trees, they discovered a lake a short distance away. When they reached it, they stood under a massive oak. Its heavy branches and foliage kept the ground under it dry. He lowered the umbrella. They watched a thousand raindrops strike the face of the lake.

Steven said, "The first year of our marriage was wonderful. I remember how I felt. I felt complete."

"Yes. I did, too."

"We used to sleep in the same bed and eat all our meals in the ComRoom."

"And talk and talk."

"That was allowed, the first year. Then we stopped. Just like that. As if it had never happened."

"That was what we were supposed to do."

The raindrops assaulted the lake water. The wind hissed angrily.

Steven said, "I want us to try. I think we should try."

Marian nodded.

She looked into his eyes. She put her arms around his neck and kissed his lips.

She said, "I still love you."

She took the umbrella from him and threw it into the lake. Then she kissed him again, open-mouthed.

She leaned back and said, "You know how I feel now?"

He looked into her eyes and, as the grayness dissolved in the sudden heat, he knew exactly what she meant when she said, "Wet!"

THE WORD

Ben Forrester was a typical star-trader, who could rattle off all the reasons for space exploration: finding new sources of raw materials, terraforming planets so you could colonize them, and then build factories or develop agribusinesses, etc., etc., etc. In short, for Ben Forrester, space travel was a great way to make money. But he could care less about pursuing knowledge, or discovering alien life forms, or studying the remains of extinct, extraterrestrial civilizations in far-flung star systems.

If you asked him, he would say, "Give me a dead planet any day, so I can get right down to business. Otherwise, I'll have to deal with ecologists, astrobiologists, archeologists, sociologists, and all the other ologists. Not to mention the worst pests of all: the *cryptos*."

Max Fischer was one of those pests that star-traders called cryptos—that is, he was a "cryptoanalytic linguist." Whenever a starship found an inhabited planet, or even one on which there were traces of what looked like an extinct intelligent species, one of the first specialists on the scene was a crypto, whose assignment was to find and study and master the local spoken and/or written language(s).

Max's assignments had been few and far between. It was almost forty years since the invention of hyperchannels—self-created wormholes that transformed light-years of astronomical distance into two- or three-day hops. And in those forty years of interstellar exploration, hundreds of planets had been visited. But in the chaotic, unpredictable soup of the universe, the ingredients for life rarely chanced to be in the right place at the right time. So most of the new worlds were barren—too near a sun, or too far, not the right mix of elements, too much deadly radiation.

And when life *was* discovered, the variables were remarkable. There were so many different ways to build organic matter, with or without carbon. There were just as many ways for an organism to feed itself. And genetic codes could be written in vastly different biochemical formats. But there was one constant—one key to life: water. It might be trapped in underground pools. Or it might flow down periodically from melting ice caps to awaken organisms that had slept for decades. But unless there was water at some time, *liquid* water, there was no life.

And when a planet was squeezed dry by climate change, or a burst of solar heat, life was squeezed out of it, too.

There was another rule that seemed to apply to living things. Whenever a creature emerged that not only made copies of itself and changed its environment, but also realized that it existed, it inevitably, inexorably, developed language.

When star-traders arrived too late, among the dead fragments and tantalizing shards of an alien past they usually found histories or mythologies written (on stone, or metal, or whatever else was available) in forgotten languages. There were no Rosetta stones to help search out the meanings of the symbols. But the cryptos were often able to solve those mysteries.

Six times, Earth explorers found life that was still living. Three of those encounters were with unthinking creatures—things driven by alien instincts, fascinating to astrobiologists, but as remote to thought as an amoeba or an oak tree.

Three times, the star-traders met beings that met *them*. That's what had happened five years ago, on the fourth planet circling Procyon A. And Max Fischer was the crypto on duty.

Ben Forrester asked him, "What were they like? Interesting? Dangerous?"

He and Max were enjoying cold beers at an open-air saloon on the planet *Dertuy-É*—a planet where the open air was actually breathable.

Max smiled nostalgically and said, "They called themselves the *N'bbay*, although it took me a long time to find that out. They were very tall—eight or nine feet tall—and they came in all kinds of shapes and colors, with an assortment of appendages and attachments. Each of them had what appeared to be a head in approximately the same place. They weren't very pretty. And they weren't very friendly, either."

"Did you have to defrag a few?" he asked, pointing his thick index finger at Max and imitating the soft sounds of a defragmenter: "Ping, ping, ping."

Max frowned. He was slender, red-haired, in his early thirties, and not the kind of person who would ever think of defragging anybody, let alone an alien. On the other hand, Ben was a beefy fifty-year-old who (Max thought) probably had defragged someone, sometime, somewhere. Or at least, seriously considered doing it.

Max said, "They kept running away from us, screaming loudly, and blowing air out of long tubes that popped out of their bodies every now and then. And when they were frightened or angry, they had this habit of attaching themselves to each other in strange patterns, dozens of them. It was like watching some kind of bizarre acrobatic act. But they had no weapons and they never tried to hurt us."

"You figured out their language?"

"Yes. I observed them, recorded the sounds they made and how they made them, and analyzed all of that information. But of course, it takes more than science to do my job well," he said, with obvious professional pride. "It takes intuition—a mix of guesswork and experience, not to mention a talent for cryptograms."

"Why bother?"

"When you learn someone else's language, you learn how they think. How they see the world. How they see themselves. How they use their imaginations. How they handle their emotions. And that helps you find ways to work with them, bargain with them—and *trade* with them."

"What did you learn about the—what were they called?"

"The N'bbay."

Max looked up at the hazy, purple sky, watched three tiny moons race much too quickly from east to west, and thought for a moment.

Then he said, "After almost two Earth years of work, I solved the N'bbay puzzle. Yes, they were a touchy, hostile race, but who could blame them? There were six N'bbay sexes, and each of the sexes mistrusted the other five. Except for the mating season—about a month every two Earth years—they argued all the time, and fought over food and shelter and virtually everything else. But during that one month, they lusted after each other so hotly that they mated endlessly, in exhausting six-sex combinations, trading partners constantly, with two of the sexes laying thousands of eggs all over the place."

He leaned forward and brushed his fingers through his thick, red hair.

He said, "There was so much sexual hostility that each of the sexes spoke a separate, distinct language, all derived from some common *ur*-language of the past, but now much different from one another. At mating time, they used another common language to communicate, but it consisted of only a few simple phrases: 'Here!' 'Now!' 'Yes!' 'More!' And words for the numbers 'one' through 'six.'"

"Did they help you learn their languages?"

"Yes, because I managed to earn their trust."

"How did you do that?"

"I practiced, over and over, until I was able to pronounce their word for yesterday—*k'l'mm'ses'tet*—a word with four glottal stops—four clicks in the back of your throat. That won them over. And once we were able to communicate, they were willing to trade with us—they exchanged valuable minerals (which had absolutely *no* value, as far as they were concerned) for vegetables, grains and fruit trees that we adapted, genetically, to grow on their planet. Eating is their *other* vice. They're really into food. So, it was a fair exchange."

Max ordered another beer and added, "But, as the N'bbay would say, that was k'l'mm'ses'tet. Today I've got another problem to solve: the Dertuy-É."

Ben said, "Last week, you said that you were practically finished."

"I was. I am. But there's still one piece missing. And it may be the most important piece."

Ben frowned and said, "I don't think they're worth the trouble. They're the most miserable bunch of losers I've ever seen. They have no pride, no ambition. They've been around for thousands of years, but look at the way they live—in little, isolated family groups, growing just enough food to stay alive. Why not just ignore them? We've got business to do here, and I'm certain they really don't care what we do."

Max shook his head.

He said, "That's the way it seems. That's the way they are today. And I would accept that and move on. Except for what I've read on *Marju-Ma*—what we call Stone Mountain."

"I'm all ears," Ben said.

"There's a huge cave up there, with artificial walls made of some stuff that must have been invented by them centuries ago. It doesn't decay, it doesn't rust. It's as clean and shiny as if it had been carved last week. They didn't tell us about the carvings, and when someone accidentally found them, they said that what was written in the cave was mythology—stories about a world that never was. I've read the carvings, and I'm sure that what I'm reading is the history of these people."

"Thousands of years of barely surviving?"

"No, Ben, just the opposite. There were great civilizations here. They built huge cities. They were ruled by kings and emperors. They were scientists and poets and warriors."

"I don't believe it."

"It's true. I'm sure of it."

"What the hell happened to them?"

"That's the last piece of the puzzle—the piece I haven't been able to fit into place."

Max leaned back in his chair and studied the purple sky. He drank some beer.

He said, "According to the story in the cave, there was a terrible war hundreds of years ago, a savage, merciless war that killed almost everyone. And when it was over, the survivors began to live the way the Dertuy-É live today. Hand-to-mouth. No tribes, no cities, no culture. Because that's the way they *wanted* to live."

"Why?"

"That's what I've got to find out. I think the key to it is a word that appears only once in all the hundreds of lines on the cave walls, near the end of the story, when everything falls apart. It's written much larger than any other word, but it doesn't seem to be in the same language. The syllables don't fit together properly. It can't be pronounced—not according to the

Dertuy-É rules of pronunciation. And when I ask them about it, they tell me that it's not a word. It can't be spoken. Or, to translate them literally, it's a 'negative word.' I know that they're lying to me."

Ben shrugged and said, "Cities? Kings? Those lazy bums? Sounds like make-believe to me."

Max finished his beer and said, "I couldn't sleep last night. Or the night before. I keep thinking about that word. And I may have come up with the answer."

"Tell me about it."

Max stood up, reached into his pocket, pulled out some star-trader scrip and left it on the table.

He said, "Not yet. I still have some work to do on it. If I'm right, you'll be the first to know."

Ben nodded and said, "I can hardly wait."

Max had been on Dertuy-É for almost a year. His office was a desk and computer in his living quarters, a square, two-room, hardsteel cabin in the star-trader complex.

A half hour after his conversation with Ben Forrester, Max sat at his PC and scrolled down his transcription of the carvings on Stone Mountain until he came to the Word. (Lately, he had begun to think of it that way, as the Word, with a capital "W".)

The Dertuy-É language used a syllabary alphabet, in which each symbol represented a syllable: *der, mat, y-É*. There were also some seemingly unrelated symbols, whose pronunciation you had to memorize. Max assumed that these were the surviving relics of a more ancient, more prestigious language, a parallel to the way Chinese symbols were adapted by the Japanese. The carvings, like all Dertuy-É texts, were arranged in vertical columns and used what linguists call boustrophedon writing: the first line was written from the top of the page to the bottom; the second line, from the bottom to the top, with the symbols in reverse order. The third line went from top to bottom again.

Max scanned the lines quickly, stopping occasionally to review a section, or confirm his translation. When he reached the final ten lines, he read slowly, carefully, and translated what he read in a quiet, almost reverent voice.

"And this was the time (that) the Clear-Eyed Emperor of the Valley Nations feared for the life of his people. Enemies were all around them. Enemies set fire to their homes and murdered their children. And this was the time (that) he, the Clear-Eyed Emperor of the Valley Nations, climbed to the summit of the Gray-Peaked Mountain that touches the Moons, and slept(?) for many star-rises and star-falls."

Max wondered, "Maybe the Emperor wasn't sleeping. Maybe he was in some kind of trance or on a vision quest."

"And while he slept, there came to him a Messenger from Somewhere Else. And the Messenger from Somewhere Else whispered a new word to him. And the Clear-Eyed Emperor of the Valley Nations heard that new word. And he arose from his sleep. And he spoke that word. And the word was . . ."

The word was the Word. And after the Word, there were only a few more lines of history:

"And when the Clear-Eyed Emperor spoke that new word, the Dark Time descended on the world, and there was only pain and death everywhere, pain and death everywhere, pain and death everywhere. And in the world's Dark Time, every one of us died, every one of us but a few. And they, the few who did not die, turned away from the word forever, and would never see the word or know the word or say the word again, forever."

Max scrolled back to the Word. It was made up of six familiar syllables, but it was impossible to put those sounds together: a nasalized whine; two percussive, inhaled, throaty tones, the first one higher in pitch than the second; a growling puff of air; a soft whistle, accompanied by a deep undertone; and a harsh sound that resembled the "*ch*" at the end of the German "*ach*."

The Dertuy-É called it a "negative word." Max's eye moved up and down the lines of the carvings.

He thought, *Up and down. Negative and positive?*

The line in which the Word appeared was written from the top to the bottom.

Max thought, "Suppose they consider the lines going from the top to the bottom as positive lines, and the lines going from bottom to top as negative lines. They told me that the Word is a negative word. But in the carvings on the wall, it's written *positively*, from the top to the bottom. A negative word written in a positive direction. Impossible to pronounce that way. Maybe I should try to pronounce it *negatively*—backwards."

He clicked a few keys and transferred the Word, by itself, to an empty screen. He entered a couple of commands and the symbols were shifted into reverse order.

He rehearsed the sounds silently, in his mind. He smiled. They fit together perfectly now. He could say the Word.

He said it.

In a single fraction of a second, everything changed.

He felt an enormous surge of power, unimaginable power, limitless power, limitless energy. His mind exploded out of his body, which was suddenly only a memory. He could no longer be confined to flesh and blood and bone.

He soared out of the star-trader complex and into the purple sky of Dertuy-É, piercing clouds, rushing toward the airless emptiness of space. A moment later, he was chasing the planet's tiny moons, playing tag with them—close enough to touch the craters in their pock-marked crusts.

Not breathing. Not needing to breathe. He was energy, pure energy. He was mind, pure mind. He was power, pure power.

And yet, he was Max Fischer, too.

He thought, "In the beginning was the Word, and the Word was with God, and the Word was God."

He raced toward the star that was Dertuy-É's sun and fearlessly plunged through its blazing face and into the nuclear furnace at its core, bathing himself in its fierce hellfires.

How long did he stay there? He didn't know. Time was irrelevant now. He was beyond the reach of time.

Back in space again, he paused, and the part of him that was still Max thought, "Am I a god? Or am I God Himself? Was the Word what the ancient Greeks spoke to become Cronus or Zeus or Athena? And the biblical legends of giants in the earth—men and women who lived hundreds of years—prophets and seers—had they all spoken the Word?"

It was difficult for him to contain the energy he felt, to control the hunger to use his power. He looked at the stars around him in a new way—as if they belonged to him.

But the part of him that was still Max thought, "The Dertuy-É carvings say that a Messenger spoke the Word to the Emperor of the Valley Nations. A Messenger from whom? From where? Who was the God of our world? Did someone who had spoken the Word find our Earth millennia ago, spinning lifelessly in space, and create the birds and beasts and people? Did he regret what he had created, and send the Flood? Did his anger turn him into what people call the Devil?"

In the beginning was the Word . . .

Max thought, "What did the Word bring to the Dertuy-É? It brought the Dark Time, pain, death. Why? And when the Dark Time was over, the survivors turned away from the Word—forever. Why?"

It was becoming more and more difficult for Max to fight the hunger to unleash his power, to use it for the sheer pleasure of using it. It was as if the hunger itself was a kind of power.

Then Max understood why the Word had brought the Dark Time. The Emperor wasn't the only one who knew the Word. Others had spoken it. And in the wars on Dertuy-É, gods had fought with each other—gods who had been men, who were now drunk with their newfound power, and used it indiscriminately.

Max could feel that intoxication, too, and he knew that it would soon overwhelm him. He would have the power of God, but not the wisdom.

It wouldn't take long for that to happen. He could feel his mind, Max's mind, shrinking, withering, crushed under the weight of the Word.

In the beginning was the Word . . .

He hovered in space, wrapped in a whirlwind of energy, ready to give himself up to the Word, to soar forever among the stars, to fashion new worlds, to search the farthest reaches of the universe.

The Dark Time descended on the world . . .

The part of him that was still Max said the Word again.

He was sitting at his PC. He was slender, red-haired, in his early thirties.

He thought, "I'll tell the star-traders not to worry about the natives of this world. As Ben says, they don't really care what we do."

The image of the Word, in reverse, was on the screen. He erased it.

When he wrote his report, he provided a grammar and dictionary of the Dertuy-É language, and identified the Word as an ancient symbol that was untranslatable. There were so many more interesting worlds to explore that no one ever paid much attention to the language of the lazy, primitive Dertuy-É.

Max Fischer lived a long, happy life. But every now and then, when he was feeling frustrated or lonely or sad, he thought about saying the Word again. (He would never forget the sound of it.) He thought about soaring among the stars in the endless, icy reaches of space, and playing with the fires of the universe.

He thought about saying the Word again. But he never did.

THE TERMINAL PROJECT

When the train rolled up to the platform, Charles Haigeron recognized the Neuberg railroad station, although he had never been there before.

"The Central Station, with its unforgiving stone face, squats in the heart of *Die Alte Stadt*, surveying passers-by like a mother disappointed in her offspring. The architect, one of the king's favorites, had a nervous breakdown shortly after the building was completed: sadly, the signs of mental deterioration are already apparent in the design of the station. The roof is too low, and set at a peculiar slant that makes it look like an oversized hat worn at a jaunty angle. The platforms are much wider in the center than at the ends, leaving dangerous gaps at the front and rear of the trains. The benches in the waiting room are too high: when you sit on one of them, unless you are exceptionally tall, your legs dangle in the air, awkwardly—a child in a grown-up's chair. And the murals (painted by the architect himself) are thick with frantic allegorical figures rushing in all directions, as if pursued by demons, signifying who-knows-what."

Die Alte Stadt. The Old City. The heart of Neuberg, a square mile of twisted streets, once the entire city, ringed by a medieval wall, dominated by *Das Kristallschloss*—the Crystal Palace, the King's official residence. In the final years of his reign, as if he were preparing himself for the lonely exile that awaited him, the last King spent most of his time at his country home, *Kirschenwald*, in the cool, forested hills to the west.

The rest of Neuberg had grown out of its primal, central core, century after century, a slow accretive process that was accelerated when one of the Barons of Neuberg decided that he would rather be a king. So he reached out from his ancient city, absorbing distant towns and villages, swallowing up forests and fields, and casting an iron net over Austrians, Germans, Slavs and Hungarians. And when he could reach no further, he had created a new country in one small, dark corner of the world—a country that was never really a country. And, with characteristic modesty, he called it Neustria—homage to the land of Charlemagne's family.

Between the World Wars, as kingdoms and empires were rearranged and reshaped, Neuberg became a Slavic city called *Novy Gorod*. But most of its population never really accepted that change. They learned a new language, but continued to speak the old language whenever they could. And at the end of the Second World War, when national boundaries were redrawn once more, Neuberg was German again—East German. And so, before it finally ended, there was another half century of Slavic domination.

"For thousands of years, nomadic streams had surged across this backwater of the Balkans—Magyars, Slavs, Mongols, Teutons—Christians, Jews, Muslims, Pagans—leaving their imprints on language, music, liturgy, philosophy—and on the faces and the moods of the people they confronted. By the time of the First World War, the time of the last King of Neustria (though, for most of his life, he didn't know that he was the last King), Neuberg was the capital city of a country that officially spoke German, with an undercurrent of a dozen unrelated dialects and accents. Cultures mingled but never mixed, cross-pollinating each other. The arts flared brilliantly, if briefly. Hatreds simmered but never boiled. Until the Royal Engineers began to build *Der Hauptbahnhof*—the Terminal Project."

Charles paid a porter to take his trunk and suitcases off the train, hail a taxi for him and load the baggage into it.

Charles said, *"Die Brücke, bitte,"* to the driver, who nodded wordlessly.

It was a late afternoon in October, sunny and cold. There wasn't much automobile traffic. Cars and gasoline were too expensive for most Neubergers. But he could see crowds of bicyclists on the street, many of them formally dressed. And there was a steady stream of pedestrians.

Despite a constant, repetitive cycle of local conflicts, and a series of major battles against Turkey early in the twentieth century—despite two world wars and the Cold War—despite the fact that its country had disappeared—most of Neuberg itself had survived undamaged. But the gritty cobblestone streets, bleak shops, shabby row-houses and massive public buildings were gray with age, and sagging with weariness. They had seen too much suffering to believe in the Spring.

Charles Haigeron saw that same look in his own reflection every morning when he shaved. Thirty years ago, he had married his college sweetheart. Ten years ago, when the last, wispy traces of young love had soured, he and his wife had dissolved the marriage. She was a successful lawyer, who earned more than he did, so he didn't have to pay her any alimony. Their son, who had always been a stranger to Charles, blamed him, and promised never to see him again. He was true to his promise and Charles didn't miss him.

Not long after the divorce, the company he worked for was acquired by a larger competitor, and he took the generous early retirement package that was offered. The pension (plus some savings and investments) was sufficient for his needs: he remained in the apartment he and his wife had purchased on the upper West Side of Manhattan a few years after they were married, when the price was still affordable. He ate a Spartan diet, and had little interest in possessions, other than books and CDs.

For a time, he pursued a younger woman he met at a party. She was passionate, but her sexuality was distant and impersonal. To Charles, their lovemaking was too cold-blooded, like an ancient ritual with a forgotten meaning. The illusion of sex became more desirable to him than the reality. So he ended his pursuit of that pleasure.

Charles had never had close friends, even as a child. He thought that he didn't need them. He was quite comfortable walking among people without touching them or wanting to know them. But without at least one companion (even a tiresome one), or a job (even a pointless one) to fill the time, he began to lose focus. For the first time, he realized that boredom can be exhausting.

Then he saw a PBS documentary about a woman who had traced her roots back to a village in the Ukraine, from which her great-grandfather had emigrated long ago. Remarkably, she had located a distant cousin, toothless and decrepit, frozen in the timeless squalor of a country village, like an ancient dragonfly suspended in amber.

Her story reminded him of the only legacy his father had left him: a metal trunk filled with newspaper clippings, diaries and books, all of them in German. His father said that his mother, Charles's grandmother, had brought the trunk with her when she came to this country, after his grandfather's death. He read the clippings, the diaries, the books, and he was drawn into another time, another place, until that time and place became more important to him than anything else.

His grandparents had lived in Neuberg before the First World War.

After a fifteen-minute ride through a labyrinth of streets and alleys, the taxi stopped at *Die Brücke*, a cheerless, three-story inn tucked into a narrow space between a tall office building and a cluster of stores.

The taxi driver helped Charles carry his luggage into the lobby, tipped his cap when he was paid and left without speaking a word.

The front desk of the inn was four or five feet wide, enclosing an arched, low-ceilinged alcove with a narrow door in its back wall. It looked like a converted prison cell. There was no one on duty, so Charles rang the ornate brass bell that stood in one corner of the desk.

The door in the back wall opened and a slim, middle-aged woman stepped into the alcove. Her face was fine-boned and elegant. Her bright blue eyes were aggressive. And her gray hair was pulled back tightly from her face, as if to clear her field of vision.

She wore a dull, shapeless dress that hung too loosely on her narrow frame, making her look small and awkward.

"*Guten Tag*," she said.

"Good day," Charles said, in German, and continued the conversation in that language. "I am Charles Haigeron. I have a reservation. Are you Frau Geyer?"

"Yes. Did you have a pleasant trip, Herr Haigeron?"

"Yes, thank you."

She opened a drawer in the desk, took out a registration form and placed it in front of him, along with a fountain pen.

"Would you register, please?"

He filled out the form and said, "I have left the departure date open. I'm not sure when I'll be going home."

She shrugged almost imperceptibly.

"Have you ever been in Neuberg before?"

"No. But my people lived here long ago."

She seemed almost offended by his answer.

She said, "That doesn't matter, not at all. This city has changed hands so many times that it has no past. There is no history here."

"But that's why I came to Neuberg. For its history."

"You will be disappointed."

When he had completed the registration form, she turned it around to face her and studied it for a moment.

She said, "Haigeron. This is not a name I have seen before."

"Perhaps not. It doesn't sound German, does it? I don't know where we came from originally."

"That doesn't matter, either."

She handed him a key, pointed toward a narrow, dark staircase in the corner of the lobby and said, "Your room is on the second floor. I have no one to help you with your luggage."

"I'll manage. Is there a restaurant you could recommend, nearby, where I could have dinner later?"

"The Black Swan is down the street, two or three blocks, in that direction. Nothing fancy, mind you. But the food is good and it's not expensive."

"That sounds fine, Frau Geyer. Eating is just an obligation for me, not a pleasure."

"If you are not seeking pleasure, Neuberg is the perfect place for you, Herr Haigeron."

She almost smiled, then turned, opened the door behind the desk and left him alone.

His room was surprisingly spacious and tastefully furnished. The double bed was covered with a beautiful, darkly-patterned blanket. There was a tall window opposite the bed, looking out onto the street. The heavy curtains that covered it had been pulled back and tied with thick, decorative cords. A massive chest of drawers, topped with a square mirror, shared the back wall with a large closet. In the opposite corner of the room was an overstuffed, comfortable-looking chair, with a standing lamp alongside it. The bathroom was long and narrow. The sink, toilet and bathtub were ancient, but clean.

Charles had to make two trips up and down the stairs to get his luggage to his room.

He took off his coat and threw it on the bed. He didn't turn on the lamp. He didn't unpack. He sat down in the chair and stared at the cold light streaming through the window.

He was pleased. His long journey had ended. He was where he wanted to be. He was *her* guest. All of the studying, all of the preparation, was over.

Now, if he could uncover just a few more clues, he would confirm his suspicions. He would solve the mystery his grandfather had failed to solve: why the Terminal Project had never been completed.

At the Black Swan that evening, he drank a stein of bittersweet, dark beer, ate a small part of a too-generous helping of spicy ham and potato pancakes, and planned his first full day in Neuberg.

He would visit the Terminal tomorrow. But first he would go to the Art Museum, to confirm what his grandfather had written in his diary:

"*November 23, 1912*. A painter named Hans Müller, who prefers to be called Hans Mond, or even just Mond: there is an image of the moon in every one of his paintings. Not especially talented, but his canvases please the eye. I wandered through his show at Leibmann's gallery, reviewed it for my column—a favorable review, of course, because he's the darling of the Royal family. But his work disturbs me. Up close, very close, when I studied his brush strokes, there was *something* just beneath the surface. (Did I imagine it? No. It appeared in every painting. I'm sure of it.) A thin, barely perceptible web—lines so faint that they were almost invisible—hidden within the bland planes of color, in the smiling moon, everywhere. I shiver when I remember it. A fierce rumble of thunder on a sunny, cloudless day. The first tremors of an earthquake in Eden. Corruption at the core of banality. Why?"

"*June 3, 1913*. A newly popular young landscape artist, Heinrich Bär: an echo of Mond? An excellent draftsman. Listless, lazy scenes. Cows in the pasture, chickens in the barnyard, stolid, cheerful peasants, lazy aristocrats. Strong design. Bold, clumsy brushstrokes. And just beneath the surface, an almost invisible web, woven by a phantom spider. Mond. Bär. Are there others, as well?"

What if his grandfather was wrong? What if there were no spiderwebs in those paintings? What if all the hints, all the clues, were simply the imaginings of an unhealthy mind.

Charles knew little about his grandfather. His grandmother rarely spoke of him, and when she did, she always said the same things: he was a marvelous writer. Everyone read his newspaper column, which he called *Die Biene* (The Bee) because it punctured pretense with the sting of satire. But, Grandma insisted, he was never cruel. And he was a favorite of the King and His Majesty's family.

She never talked about him as a person. It was as if she had never lived with him; as if she knew him only the way others did—by his work.

He had died before she left Neuberg, a few weeks after the War began. How did he die? Why did she leave?

Tomorrow, at the art museum, he would try to look through the eyes of his grandfather at Neuberg, the way it was a century ago. What would he see?

Charles drank his beer slowly, deliberately. When he finished it, he ordered another.

What would he see?

That night, soothed by several steins of beer, he slept dreamlessly.

In the morning, he awoke rather late: it was almost 8:30.

He struggled with the shower. The water was either too hot or too cold.

The light over the bathroom mirror was dim. When he shaved, he would have missed a few spots if he hadn't felt the stubble with the tip of his finger.

Before he left his room, he studied a map of Neuberg, on which he had marked several locations.

When he walked through the lobby on his way to the street, Frau Geyer was perched behind the front desk, making entries in an account book.

She looked up, said, "Good day, Herr Haigeron," and went back to her work.

A few blocks from the Inn, Charles found a sleek storefront coffee shop called *Die SchnelleKüche*—a flash of modernity in an old-world setting.

The Fast Kitchen, he thought. *Fast food, I guess*.

He ordered *cafe au lait* and a croissant. The coffee was very strong. The croissant was large and tasteless.

The museum was a long walk away, across the center of the Old City. Even during a work day, there were few cars in the street, but there were hordes of bicycles and pedestrians. The people walked and cycled quickly, but their faces reflected little excitement or interest. Most wore drab, unfashionable clothing, although the younger men and women tended to be a little more stylish.

It was 10:15 when he arrived at the museum. He was much too early. It didn't open for another forty-five minutes. So Charles walked down to the broad river—the *Mühlestrom*—that cut the city, east to west, into two almost equal halves. Three bridges spanned the water. One was built during the thirteenth century, the other two during the nineteenth. Charles sat in a small park near the oldest bridge and looked across the river at the Crystal Palace, a huge, rococo structure that looked too delicate to sustain its own weight.

Though he had never been there, Charles thought that he knew the layout of the palace well enough to guide tourists through it. His grandfather had been there many times and had described it in his columns and in his diary.

Charles could picture the king and queen at a banquet in the Great Hall, or receiving guests in the Crimson Gallery. And there was Crown Prince Ferdinand beside them, in his early thirties, tall and handsome and charming, said to be the most eligible bachelor in Europe.

In one diary entry, Charles's grandfather had written:

"To a satirist like me, the Crown Prince poses a problem. There are times when satire must be mute. Yesterday, at the premiere of Goldwasser's dreadful new operetta, *The Duke of Thessaly*, the audience ignored the stage and watched the Prince. By a look or a smile, he makes us feel as if he cares about us—loves us. And we return that love a thousand-fold, a million-fold. Isn't that foolish of us? Of *me*?"

Charles smiled at the satirist's discomfort. And his gullibility.

He walked back to the museum. A few minutes after 11:00, a few minutes late, it opened. He paid the entrance fee, asked for the location of three paintings and walked quickly to the gallery where they were displayed.

Springtime #6, Hans Müller (also known as Hans Mond), 1912.

Donated by the Löwenstein Family

It was a large, semi-abstract canvas, painted in broad, flat planes of warm color that caressed the eyes. The shapes vaguely suggested houses, a road, a wagon—and the moon, of course. A pleasing picture.

Charles hesitated. This was the first test. He wondered what he would do if his grandfather failed the test.

He moved toward the painting, slowly, cautiously. When he was only a few inches from it, he scanned the featureless planes of color.

He smiled.

A faint spiderweb of lines spread just below the surface of the painting, almost imperceptibly, hidden in the brushstrokes, peeking out from the golden face of the full moon.

"Corruption at the core of banality."

Another painting by Mond hung alongside this one. And it, too, was bound with an almost invisible web.

On the far wall of the gallery, Charles found Heinrich Bär's *Chloe in the Afternoon*, a flattering portrait of an elegant lady on the terrace of a country estate.

Up close, in the folds of her flowered, silken dress—in the strands of her golden hair—in the branches of the tall trees that surrounded her: a hidden spiderweb.

Karl Haigeron was right about the painters. He was undoubtedly right about all of the other clues.

He had made only one critical mistake, and Charles intended to correct it.

The Terminal Project.

A block-square excavation, a shattered foundation wall, a grid of massive, rusted beams, guarded by a four-foot-high, steel-mesh fence.

Charles's fingers gripped the thick, cold wires of the fence.

Why had it been preserved, he wondered. *As a monument to failure? As a reminder to Kings that kingdoms are fragile?*

After all the time he had spent reading about it, learning about it, he was disappointed. The wreckage seemed trivial, barren, empty of meaning.

There was a small, bronze plaque set in a weathered, concrete pillar in front of the fence:

The site of the Neuberg Railroad Terminal. Groundbreaking began in Spring, 1913. Construction interrupted by labor unrest and acts of sabotage. At the outbreak of War in August 1914, the Project was suspended and never completed.

And if it had been completed in time, would it have saved Neustria?

"***Die Biene***—*September 8, 1912*

"The other night, at an after-theater party, I gathered my courage, took a deep breath and asked Field Marshall Erich von Massenbach a ticklish question: 'Is the Neuberg Terminal Project really worthwhile? Couldn't we find a better way to spend all of that money?'

"In case you've never met him, I should point out that the Field Marshall is every inch the soldier: much taller than I am, handsome, straight as an arrow, confident—a born leader.

"He looked down at me, smiled patiently and said, 'We must avoid fighting tomorrow's wars with yesterday's weapons. On tomorrow's battlefields, armies will be enormous. And the machinery of war that supports them will be enormous, too—artillery, ammunition, food, forage for the horses. And everything will have to be moved from place to place, from front to front, much more quickly. We are a land-locked country. We are surrounded by shifting alliances. Today's ally is tomorrow's antagonist. Our enemies may attack us from any direction. So we must be able to mobilize more quickly, move our armies more quickly, supply them more quickly.

That's why we're rebuilding our railroad network. And that's why we need a central Terminal that can manage the network efficiently. Is it worthwhile to spend all that money to defend our nation? Do you doubt it?'

"How can I disagree with the Field Marshall? I am certainly not a student of military strategy. And I know even less about railroads. He is a hero of two wars, the Supreme Commander of our armies, and the King has called him, the 'Protector of the Kingdom.'

"Is the Neuberg Terminal Project really worthwhile?

"It is, gentle reader. It is."

"September 9, 1912.

"The arrogance of Massenbach! 'Tomorrow's battlefields.' Will there *be* a tomorrow? Are we a nation, or have we become the ghost of a nation? Our King spends less and less time in Neuberg. He lets his Chancellor rule the country, while His Majesty plays house with his mistress at the Kirschenwald. And the Royal Court follows suit, hunting, sailing, feasting, dancing—but never governing. And all the while, the city—the countryside—seethe with unrest. I hear a Babel of angry words every day, in a dozen languages. And there stands the noble Protector of the Kingdom, overstuffed, overfed and overly satisfied with himself. I could have said, Never mind the enemies outside our borders. Beware of the enemies *within*, my lord. But after all, isn't that how you fashioned your reputation? In '06, by crushing the peasant uprisings in the *UnterBerge*? And three years ago, when you marched into the National Assembly and arrested Groener and Litzmann—because they had become dangerous revolutionaries—because they had dared to say the word 'Democracy' in public. Look around you, my Lord Protector of the Kingdom. Listen. Listen carefully. There is something afoot—*something*. Watch your step. There's a deadly spiderweb being woven around you with threads of steel. There's an undercurrent, a whisper, a murmur. And it grows, hour by hour, day by day. There are signs of it everywhere, if you look for them. But the King is at his country home. The Field Marshall is at the theater. The Crown Prince is at the concert hall. The music drowns out the whispers. But when the music stops, listen, *listen*: you can still hear the whispers."

That evening, as he left the inn for dinner, Charles stopped at the front desk to speak to Frau Geyer.

He said, "I wonder if you could help me, Frau Geyer?"

"If I can, certainly."

"I'd like to search for some information in official records—police reports, court proceedings—going back almost a century."

"I doubt if very much has survived, with all we've been through."

"Perhaps you are right, but I'd like to try. Do you know anyone who might be able to help me: someone in the government, perhaps?"

Frau Geyer looked down at the desk-top, as if she were studying a chessboard.

When she looked up again, she said, "I know someone who may be able to help you. I'm not sure if he would be interested in doing so. He used to be a police inspector, but he's retired now. His name is Otto Berndt. He knows *everyone*."

"How can I get in touch with him?"

"I'll call him. I'll let you know what he says."

Charles smiled.

"Thank you," he said, began to turn away, and then looked back at Frau Geyer and added, "I wonder if he knows anyone at the Town Hall in Berndorf. That's not far from here, is it?"

"Berndorf? No, it isn't far. It is a suburb of the city—a rather dreary place. You can take the Number Seven bus to get there."

"Perhaps you know someone there I can speak to?"

"No. Why would I?"

"You were born in Berndorf, weren't you? You grew up there."

Frau Geyer's bright blue eyes watched his face for a moment before she answered him.

"Why do you know that?"

"I told you that I'm interested in history."

"What are you looking for in Berndorf?"

"Marriage records."

Frau Geyer shrugged. "I have not lived there in many years. I do not know anyone there. I will call Inspector Berndt for you."

"Many thanks, Frau Geyer."

As he walked out, he heard her lift the telephone receiver and dial.

"**Die Biene**—May 1, 1913

"Today, gentle reader, the Bee will sting no one. On the contrary, I feel that I must confess to a 'weakness' which is shared by so many of my countrymen: I love Traps! And Miguel Sanchez is *my* hero, too!

"Traps. Liebkind has called it the 'Dance of Death.' But Sanchez himself denies this, calling Traps the 'Dance of Life.' He says, 'It isn't about dying: it's about *defying* Death, laughing in His bony face, watching Him lunge at you, hearing Him whistle past, and never letting Him touch you. When I play, I play for Life. Death is for losers.'

"Traps. Two three-man teams on a walled-in, jai-alai court, the front wall a transparent mesh of steel that protects us while we watch them. The *cesta,* a curved basket-shaped racket strapped to the player's forearm. The *pelota*, smaller and harder than the jai-alai ball. The leaping, twisting ballet, as the ball is thrown, explodes off the wall, ricochets, rebounds, is caught in mid-air and hurled against the wall again.

"Traps. Jai-alai, but *not* jai-alai. For we have added something special to the game, something the Basques never thought of: the Pass.

"Imagine it with me. See it in your mind's eye, as you have seen it a hundred times at the Traps Arena, holding your breath, as thousands of others hold their breaths. Two or three times a game, the server stands at the yellow line, only twelve feet from the front wall, in the center channel. And when he serves, he faces the small yellow circle on the wall directly in front of him, five feet above the ground. He sets himself, crouches, raises the cesta far above his head, the pelota cradled in it. He reaches back and, in one lightning motion, throws the ball into the circle and lunges forward. The ball instantly recoils from the wall, a leather-covered bullet, a few feet from the ground, eager to punish the server for his arrogance. But—usually—not always—the server is gone, spread-eagled on the ground, safe from harm. The Pass. No one else can touch the ball. The server has scored ten points for his team. And he has danced with Death—and Life.

"Sanchez, of course, is the Master of the Pass. He has Passed six times in one game. No one else has had the courage to try that—or the skill to succeed. Some have been injured. Some have died.

"Should we feel guilty about loving our game so much—a game that plays with Death?

"No, gentle reader, I think not. I agree with Sanchez: Traps is the game of Life."

Charles spent most of the next day in his room, reviewing his notes, planning his next moves, and waiting for Frau Geyer to get back to him about her friend, Inspector Berndt. Late in the afternoon, she called.

"Herr Haigeron, I have spoken to Otto Berndt. He says that he will try to assist you as best he can."

"Thank you. Shall I call him to arrange a meeting?"

"No need. He lives not far from here. I suggested that he meet you for dinner tonight at the Black Swan. Perhaps I shouldn't have made that arrangement without asking you first?"

"No, no. I'm pleased that you did."

"He'll be there at seven this evening."

"Thank you again, Frau Geyer."

"My pleasure," she said.

Inspector Otto Berndt (retired) was a short, bald, heavy-set man in his late sixties. He wore a sober, dark suit and a surprising red tie. He puffed on a heavily-carved, wooden pipe, biting thoughtfully on the worn stem and releasing clouds of smoke periodically. His face was square and ruddy, his gray eyes seemed friendly, and his expression was calm and pleasant.

Charles rose to greet him and extended his hand, which was grasped firmly, almost painfully, as they shook hands.

After Inspector Berndt had ordered a stein of beer, Charles said, "Frau Geyer says that you have offered to help me, Herr Berndt. I'm grateful to you."

"Well, I am not sure how much I can do for you. But my days are rather empty since I retired. I could use a little excitement."

He smiled.

"I'm not sure if 'excitement' is the right word, Herr Berndt. I'd like you to help me find some very old documents."

"Documents?"

"Yes. Police reports. Trial records. All of them from the years before the First World War."

Herr Berndt puffed a few times. "That may be quite difficult. If, in fact, those documents still exist."

His beer arrived and he sipped a few mouthfuls while he contemplated the task ahead of them.

Then he said, "I like to think, professionally speaking, that I'm a very logical man. So let's begin at the beginning. Tell me, in broad terms at least, what you're after. What are we searching for?"

Charles hesitated, but only for a moment.

He said, "My grandfather lived in Neuberg before the war—the First World War—when this was still Neustria. He was a writer—a newspaper columnist. Not long after the war started, he died, or was killed—I don't know which. His wife, my grandmother, came to America with her two-year-old son, my father. I knew her when I was growing up. She was very beautiful, and very proud—too proud to make the mistakes that people make when they're practicing a new language. So, through all the years she was in America, she never really tried to master English. She knew enough to get along, but she spoke only German when she had a choice. With us, for example. She lived in my father's house like a stranger—remote, quiet, keeping to herself. She died when I was ten."

"And you want to know more about her, and your grandfather? Is that it?"

Charles shook his head and said, "No. I want to finish a job that my grandfather began."

Herr Berndt raised his eyebrows, tilted his head to one side and waited for Charles to explain.

"I have a collection of his newspaper columns and I have his diaries, too. In the years just before the war, he began to suspect that there was a group here in Neuberg that was working undercover, against the government."

"I'm sure there were many such groups. Neustria was a make-believe country, after all—a pastiche of nationalities that had very little in common, except for their hatred of the royal family."

"But one group, in particular, had caught my grandfather's attention."

"*Which* group?"

"He never named it. But he found clues to it everywhere."

"What kind of clues?"

Charles tasted his own beer, savored it.

He said, "He wasn't a detective, of course. But because he was such a popular writer, he had access to virtually everyone in Neuberg—in the arts, in business, and in the government—including the royal family. He watched. He listened. He observed. And he began to find those clues."

"For example?"

"I am sure that, as a policeman, you won't be persuaded by what he discovered."

Herr Berndt pursed his lips and said, "You would be surprised how much of detection is about feelings, rather than facts. You know, Einstein said that his discoveries came to him from an intuitive leap that he later fleshed out with reasoning. He had no bias against intuition. Nor have I."

The waiter cautiously interrupted them. They ordered dinner.

Charles said, "My grandfather noticed that a new kind of joke was making the rounds. Although the stories were different, they all had one thing in common: the characters were intelligent animals, philosophical animals, highly educated animals, and they were all carnivores—lions, bears, tigers, foxes, wolves. He couldn't trace the origin of these jokes, but he heard them everywhere."

Herr Berndt said, "Animals. Carnivores."

"He made note of it in his diaries. He wondered about it. Then he found something else that surprised him. Some very popular artists were playing a strange game: their paintings seemed innocent, but there was something evil in them, just below the surface, literally. Mond and Bär, for example. I looked at their work a couple of days ago here at the Art Museum, and it's true."

"*What* is true?"

"There is a tiny spiderweb of lines in their pictures, an undercurrent of darkness in the light. My grandfather saw this, too."

Charles sipped his beer again, then added, "And then, of course, he underlined Bär's name—Bear."

"Of course."

"He saw so many things going wrong, so many signs that the framework was falling apart. He wrote that Neustria had a King who was too lazy to govern. A National Assembly that was too frightened to take control. Political parties that were too weak to lead. And what were the people doing? He said that they were at the Traps Arena, hoping to see someone die. Or they were watching the latest show at the *Zorntheater*—the Theater of Anger—mocking morality, ridiculing love and decency. Then there were the religious fanatics, the Listeners, who were speaking in tongues that only they could understand. 'And as the winter dies,' he wrote, 'every three years, they all come to the Carnival at Jena—we all come—to feed our appetites until we can hunger no more.' That is what my grandfather wrote in his diary."

"And this *group*? Where were they, while all this was going on?"

"Here, there, everywhere, nowhere. Then, when the Terminal Project was announced, my grandfather knew what to expect."

The waiter reappeared with their entrees.

Herr Berndt cradled his pipe in the ashtray, welcomed his food with a hearty mouthful or two, then said, "He expected strikes, sabotage and the like? Why blame all that on a special group of conspirators? Wasn't there already enough turmoil in the country—enough agitation from the Slavs and Hungarians—enough pressure from the unions and the socialists and the anarchists?"

"Of course. But he believed that it was all being incited, carefully organized, channeled in one direction: to overthrow the king. The Terminal Project was the key to the king's survival. Or, at least, the group thought it was. And they wanted to make sure that he *didn't* survive."

Herr Berndt nodded and continued to eat.

Charles, who had never told anyone else about his grandfather, was exhausted. He needed a few minutes to rest. He began to eat, mechanically, hardly tasting the food.

Herr Berndt broke the silence.

"Why do you care what happened a hundred years ago in a make-believe kingdom?"

"It's unfinished business."

"Whose business? Not yours, surely."

Charles hadn't intended to explain himself to anyone. That was something he never did. But Berndt seemed to have a knack—a *policeman's* knack, perhaps—of encouraging honesty. Charles didn't trust him, and yet he told him the truth.

"You said that, in retirement, life is a little empty for you. I retired some years ago, and I felt the same way. Even when I was working, I never really enjoyed what I did. Then I found something that I *could* enjoy. When I started to read my grandfather's articles—and his diaries—I was absorbed into his world. I was challenged by what he wrote. I wanted to find out who stopped the Terminal Project. I wanted to find the truth. I read every book, every scrap of information about that time. I wanted to succeed where my grandfather had failed. To solve the puzzle, for his sake, and for mine."

"Perhaps he *did* solve the puzzle, but kept the solution to himself."

"Why would he do that?"

"I don't know."

"His diary entries just stopped, a month before the war began. He continued to write his columns for a few more weeks and then he disappeared from the newspaper, without a word of explanation from the editors. In a month or two, after the invasion and the occupation, no one cared about anything but survival. And apparently, he didn't survive."

Herr Berndt nodded.

He said, "Surviving takes a peculiar kind of talent. (I speak from experience.) Survivors don't resist the tide. We swim with it. We change color. We learn new ways to speak."

"And what *are* you after that?"

"We are what we are."

Herr Berndt studied his beer for a minute or two, then said, "With regard to your investigation, may I offer some advice?"

"Of course. I appreciate any help you can give me."

"The most important thing I learned as a policeman—and it took me some time to learn it—was to look for evidence, not confirmation. From what you have been telling me, you believe that you have already solved the mystery."

"I suppose so, but I'm not certain about it."

"So what you want to find here is confirmation. You looked at some paintings and saw what your grandfather saw. And you said to yourself, 'He was right!' Your suspicions were confirmed. But what if there is another explanation for what he saw—what *you* saw? Did you consider that possibility?"

Charles shook his head.

Herr Berndt said, "I don't mean to preach. You may, in fact, have the answer. But look at the evidence as objectively as you can. There may be more than one way to interpret it."

Herr Berndt re-lit his pipe and leaned back in his chair.

Charles said, "I'll be careful," but he was only being polite.

"So much for sermons," Herr Berndt said, smiling and liberating several thin streams of smoke. "Tomorrow, if you like, we'll visit an old friend of mine who works in the Hall of Records. He should be able to help you."

Charles raised his beer glass and toasted, "To tomorrow."

Herr Berndt raised his glass in response and echoed, "To tomorrow."

"February 14, 1913.

"In a few days, the Carnival at Jena begins. A ritual that is much less and much more than it should be. Once, it was a pagan celebration of Winter's death and the rebirth of Spring. Lurking somewhere in our racial memory, like silent shadows, are the old gods, the old rituals, the sacrifices, the primeval fear that the ice would never thaw, that the days would never grow longer, that the earth would never free itself from the cold breath of the North Wind.

"When Jesus came into our lives, the Carnival was transformed into a pre-Lenten ceremony during the six days before Ash Wednesday. And we gathered at Jena only once every three years (reflecting the Trinity, perhaps?). We were enlightened. We were saved. So we suppressed the superstitions. But the celebration never really became sensual, for we have never been a sensual people. We are afraid of passion. We crush it. Our old gods were never seductive. They fought and feuded. They tricked each other. They sought vengeance. They even died. Our religions, pagan or Christian, have always been thick-skinned and brutal. We dwell on the Crucifixion, the Passion. We can still hear the raw pounding of the nails piercing the hands of the Savior. We can still feel the hot, agonizing thrust of the Holy Lance. His death touches us far more deeply than His resurrection. It matches the coldness of our bare churches and of our bare, predestined spirits.

"Today, the Listeners feed on that coldness. They hear the voices of angry angels (they say) and the voices of the dead. They speak in those voices, in tongues only they can understand. They tell us that the voices cry out against the Carnival at Jena. And surely, if the dead look down at us, their voices *would* cry out.

"In the week before Ash Wednesday, every three years, when the frost still coats the grass, and the trees are still barren skeletons, and the fierce winds still blow from the mountains, they would see a thousand tents and wooden shacks spring up in the valley around the village of Jena, and they would see the valley become the Carnival. Once, it was a place for simple indulgences, innocent vices: too much rich food, too much wine, too much beer. Loud music, dancing under the stars. Gambling. Wild carnival rides and games. But year by year, we lost our innocence, and the Carnival is a mirror of that loss. Today, it is a nightmare—a clear, ugly reflection of what we have become. For six days, nothing is forbidden, nothing is unlawful, nothing is punished. We unleash our hungers and our passions and our angers and try to quench them. I have been there. I have seen myself reflected in that mirror. There is no darker place this side of Hell.

"The king and his court don't have to go to Jena. They have their own private Carnival, their own rituals, their own lawless lives. But they are willing to look the other way and allow us to indulge our lusts for a week. What harm can it do?

"The Listeners are angry. They are ashamed. The voices of angry angels, the voices of the dead, sing to them of sin. I hear voices, too. Of the living. In the streets, in the cafes. And they are singing the same song."

The Hall of Records smelled of the past. The same musty aroma hovered around Herr Berndt's friend, the archivist, Herr Stein. He was a tall, slender man in his early sixties. He moved precisely, economically, as if he had rationed his energy so he would never run out of it.

"We now have computers," Herr Stein said, without apparent pride, "and everything new is being entered into them. And we are converting all of the old paper records we have. That will take some time."

Charles and Herr Berndt were sitting in Herr Stein's gray, threadbare office, across the desk from him.

Herr Berndt said, "My friend is interested in looking at the records of police investigations, as well as trial transcripts from nineteen fourteen, in the months just before the War. He is particularly interested in the Terminal Project."

Herr Stein's eyes looked back in time for a minute or two, and then he said, "That may be a problem. Most of the material about the Terminal was destroyed. I'm afraid there isn't much for you to examine. I gathered it all into a few file boxes—three or four."

Charles nodded and said, "I suppose that's to be expected, after two wars."

Herr Stein shook his head.

"Actually," he said, "the wars had little to do with it. It was the king, the anger of the king. The labor unions were marching in the streets. There was rioting and looting. Neuberg was a dangerous place. And then: the sabotage of the Terminal Project. And the king was suddenly there in the streets of the city, on horseback, an avenging angel in the uniform of a soldier, sword unsheathed, leading his Royal Guardsmen. We call that time, 'The Days of Rage.'"

"Yes," Charles said, "I've read that even the people close to him were afraid of what he would do to *them*."

"He suspended all civil rights and declared martial law. He took control of the newspapers and magazines. He closed the theaters and concert halls. His troops shot the strikers, the rioters and the looters. They arrested what he called 'agitators and dissidents,' a category that seemed to cover nearly everyone. Foreign nationals were expelled from the country. The King closed the courts, replacing them with secret military tribunals, where defendants had no right to counsel, and no right to appeal. The official name for these tribunals was 'Judicial Inquiries,' but justice was nowhere to be found. He arrested anyone who had ever disagreed with the government, with him, with his ministers. Virtually every sentence was a death sentence. Old scores were settled. Old enemies were eliminated. It was a terrible time."

Herr Stein paused, breathed deeply, and continued.

"But that wasn't enough for the king. Before he went into exile, he declared war on history. He said, 'We will erase the past. Then let them try to judge us!' And he ordered every ministry, every department, every official, to destroy all of the documents about the Terminal Project. To burn them. Imagine what we lost. It was one of the critical moments in our history, and almost nothing is left. Of course, not everyone complied. Some scattered documents were saved, by local officials, or by people who managed to leave the country. And no one can really erase history: there are too many witnesses. But here in Neuberg, most of our national memory of that time was erased. And then the chaos that followed—the wars, the invasions, the occupations—simply finished the job the king had begun."

Herr Stein bowed his head slightly and held out his hands, palms up, as if he were asking for absolution.

Charles said, "Perhaps I'll find something of value in whatever remains."

Herr Stein nodded slowly and repeated, "Perhaps."

Herr Stein stood up, came around the desk and said, "Please follow me, gentlemen."

They walked behind him along two corridors, down three flights of stairs, through two doors, each of which Herr Stein unlocked with a master key, and into a high-ceilinged room filled with shelves that were packed with neatly labeled, black file boxes. Ladders with wheeled legs were attached to each row, so files on the upper shelves could be reached.

Herr Stein stopped so suddenly that Charles bumped into him.

Herr Stein pulled a ladder closer, and climbed up three rungs.

"Here," he said, and handed a file box to Charles. It wasn't as heavy as it looked. He gave a second box to Charles. Then he gestured to Herr Berndt and handed him a third.

Herr Stein said, "That's all there is."

He came down the ladder and said, "There is a room on this floor where you can examine the documents. It is very well lit."

He led them to a door in the far wall of the archive and unlocked it. He switched on the overhead lights—three bright yellow, florescent fixtures. There was a wide table in the center of the room, with several thick, wooden chairs around it.

Charles and Herr Berndt put the file boxes on the table. Herr Stein took a white slip out of his breast pocket, filled it out quickly and asked Charles to sign it.

Then he said, "Please take as much time as you like. When you've finished, dial seven-eight-eight on that phone in the corner of the room. I'll come and sign you out."

Charles thanked him and he left.

Herr Berndt said, "Would you like me to help you?"

"Thank you, Herr Berndt, but I have to look at everything with my own eyes."

He opened the first box. There were several bound volumes in it, as well as a slim stack of loose, yellowed sheets bound with a leather cord. Charles put the stack on the table, struggled with the cord for a minute or two until he could untie it, and then sat down and began to examine the documents. Herr Berndt sat next to him and opened one of the bound volumes.

Charles said, "These are handwritten lists of strikers who were arrested. They look like they were jotted down quickly by a policeman, in no special order, as the arrests were made."

He leafed through several more sheets and added, "There are police reports—summaries of activity at the Terminal site." He read, "'July 6, 1914—Construction crews walked off the job at noon, then began picketing the area. Union leaders and agitators were rounded up at their headquarters.'"

He quickly exhausted the other loose sheets and said, "Nothing of significance."

He retied the bundle and pulled a book from the box.

Herr Berndt turned the pages of the volume he was examining and said, "Official contracts with the builders of the Terminal. Deeds to the land on which the Terminal was to be built, which was purchased from individual owners by the Crown. And there are specifications, too—plans, materials, and such. Does that interest you?"

"No. But please let me see it, anyway."

In a few minutes, he had riffled through all the pages.

He said, "The cost was enormous: millions of Marks. There's nothing important here."

Charles selected another book. He said nothing as he scanned page after page. He was finished in a few minutes.

"Trivia," he said.

He closed the book, put it on the table, and took a third volume from the box. Herr Berndt watched him patiently, took each discarded volume from him and glanced through it.

There were two more bound files in the first box. They were sheaves of correspondence, primarily addressed to the king and the minister of war and Field Marshall Massenbach, from officials who were designing the

Terminal and the new railroad facilities throughout the country that would be built at the same time. There were also plans for new rolling stock and more modern, more powerful locomotives.

Charles stopped at a letter to the crown prince. It was written by Oskar Kellerman, the architect who had been chosen for the Project. Charles knew that he was a close friend of the minister of war and a frequent guest at the Crystal Palace.

Charles read the letter, then read it aloud to Herr Berndt.

"I don't have the crown prince's letter, but I have the reply. Kellerman writes, 'Please permit me to reassure Your Grace that, with the extraordinary resources that His Highness the King has placed at our disposal, and our own total commitment, we will complete this Project before the deadline. We will work on a three-shift, twenty-four-hour-a-day schedule. I have personally created a detailed, step-by-step plan that enables us to perform several tasks in parallel, so that we can drastically shorten the time the whole Project will take. I am honored that you are taking the time out of your busy schedule to visit the site tomorrow. I cannot express how much I look forward to showing you what we have already accomplished.'"

Herr Berndt said, "That letter interests you?"

"Yes. The crown prince interests me."

"May I ask why?"

Charles said, "My grandfather didn't admire much about this country, but he admired the crown prince. And apparently, that was how most people felt. I have my doubts about him."

"Doubts?"

Charles wasn't ready to show his hand.

He said, "Let me see if there are any other letters of interest here."

As the dates of the letters approached the dangerous summer when the First World War erupted, Kellerman began to worry about delays. The architect's plan was breaking down, as sudden, wildcat strikes broke out. Then the sabotage began. Building materials disappeared or were damaged. Tunnels collapsed. A shipment of rails was hijacked and destroyed. And Kellerman complained that the enemies of the Project seemed to have inside information. They were always one step ahead of him. In late July, after the final act of sabotage—a series of explosions that destroyed most of the

Terminal's foundation and superstructure—Kellerman wrote a bitter and surprisingly honest letter to the crown prince.

"Your Grace," Charles read aloud, "to see everything we planned, everything we accomplished, become nothing more than a twisted pile of wreckage, is too painful to endure. The storms of war are darkening the horizon. The deluge will soon be upon us. And the Terminal Project, our hope for weathering that deluge, is no more. It is too late, Your Grace. God help us, it is too late."

Herr Berndt said, "It was always too late. The Terminal would not have saved Neustria. We were a pigmy among giants, a footnote to the history of the War."

Charles didn't respond. He continued to look at the letters, but found nothing else of interest to him.

He replaced the contents of the first box, closed it, and opened the second box.

He found detailed progress reports on the construction of the Neuberg Terminal, and of other stations, as well as auxiliary projects—expansion and upgrading of rail lines, new traffic control centers. There was also an Army mobilization plan, over two hundred pages long, describing precisely how each military district would respond to a full alert, with a scenario covering each potential enemy or combination of enemies—where each regiment and division would assemble, how many trains were needed to transport them, what the timetable was for every movement.

Charles read a few sections to Herr Berndt, who said, "At the time of the First World War, mobilization had become a self-fulfilling prophecy—a terrible engine that couldn't be stopped, once it was started. When the political crisis came, it set off a chain reaction of mobilization, all over Europe. The process took weeks to complete, and it was irreversible. No one dared to back down, to reconsider. No one dared to think, to reason, to consider the cost. It was truly madness. And millions died. The Days of Rage, indeed."

There was nothing more of interest in the second box.

The third box had only two bound volumes in it. One contained a lengthy National Assembly evaluation of the Terminal Project, written in May, 1913, when the work had just begun. Large sections of the document, outlining the military necessity for the Terminal, were contributed by the minister of war.

The second volume was a hodge-podge of unrelated material, much of it trivial and fragmentary.

Herr Berndt wondered, "Have you found anything yet to help you solve your mystery? Any confirmation of your suspicions?"

Charles smiled, but didn't answer him.

Then he said, "Here's something."

Herr Berndt leaned forward, looking over Charles's shoulder at the handwritten document.

Charles said, "This is not the whole police report, only page three. It's signed, 'Inspector Oppenheim.'"

He read it to Herr Berndt:

"How is that supposed to help me? He doesn't deny his guilt, nor does he affirm it. He will not answer my questions. And how can I persuade him to do so? Is he at the center of it all (which is my belief), or merely an observer? Of course, I'm certain that we can persuade some of the others to tell us.

"And what if I'm right about him? What do I do then? What will the king do?

"Yesterday, when I entered his cell, he greeted me as he always does—politely, warmly. He never complains. He never seems angry. He asks me about the news, and I tell him all I know.

"When I mention the names, and the certain fate, of the others, he simply nods, as if the names, the people, and their fate have nothing to do with him.

"It should not be difficult to discover the truth. Most of his men are intelligent and well educated. Fear is usually a valuable tool with such men. But in this case, it is a two-edged tool: I fear what they will tell me about *him*."

Charles repeated the last line, aloud: "I fear what they will tell me about *him*."

"You seem quite pleased, Herr Haigeron."

Charles said, "I suppose that I am," but he actually felt uneasy, though he didn't know why.

Perhaps, he thought, *it's because I'm finally so close to the end*.

He looked at the remaining documents in the book, but found nothing else that he considered important. He closed the book, and put it back in the box.

He said, "We are finished here."

He dialed 788 on the phone, spoke to Herr Stein and sat down again to wait for him.

Herr Berndt said, "And have you found what you were looking for? To me, it seems little enough."

Charles said, "I know you won't approve of what I'm about to say. I did come here for confirmation, not for evidence. But I haven't reached my conclusions carelessly. I have studied every source of information on the Terminal Project that I could find—in libraries, universities, archives. What remains here is, as you say, little enough. And I knew that's what it would be."

"Then why did you come to Neuberg?"

"Because this is where it happened. This is where my grandfather died. This is where his country died. I wanted to close the circle. And there were things I wanted to see with my own eyes. The paintings. The Crystal Palace. The Terminal Project itself."

Herr Berndt smiled and said, "And, of course, you wanted to be certain that you had solved the mystery, eh?"

"Yes."

"Are you certain now?"

"Yes, but I have one more place to go tomorrow."

"One more place."

Charles said, "Then, if you don't mind, I'd like you to join me when I tell Frau Geyer about what I have learned."

"And why must you tell Frau Geyer?"

"She is the other reason I came to Neuberg."

Herr Berndt said, "I will be there."

It was late in the afternoon of the next day when Charles returned to the inn from Berndorf. He rang the bell on the front desk.

Frau Geyer smiled when she saw him and said, "You look quite satisfied with yourself, Herr Haigeron."

"I have just come back from Berndorf."

"Ahhh!" she said, with another smile, as if she were humoring him.

Herr Berndt sometimes spoke to him and agreed with him in the same way, as if he were a child.

He returned her smile and said, "May I impose upon your time this afternoon, or later this evening? There's something I would like to discuss with you."

She nodded.

She said, "Herr Berndt is having coffee with me right now. Would you like to join us?"

Charles wondered, *Has he been waiting for me?*

He said, "Yes, fine. I just have to get something from my room."

When he reached his room, he had a sudden impulse to pack his bags and leave at once. But that wasn't the way this was supposed to end. He had to tell her.

He went into the bathroom and washed his face with cold water. He studied his reflection in the mirror. In the dim light, it looked like the face of a stranger.

He came back downstairs a few minutes later, carrying a well-worn diary. Frau Geyer was waiting for him at an open door in the lobby, several feet from the front desk. She gestured him into her apartment and closed the door behind her.

She led him through a dimly-lit foyer and a richly-furnished dining room into a small sitting room. Along one wall, potted plants hugged a tall, wide window that looked out at a neat garden. A trio of small, pastoral paintings hung on another wall. Overstuffed chairs sat around a squat coffee table. Herr Berndt sat in front of the window, in one of the chairs, sipping coffee and eating a chocolate-covered pastry.

Herr Berndt said, "Good day, Herr Haigeron."

"Good day, Herr Berndt."

Frau Geyer invited him to be seated.

She said, "Would you like some coffee?"

"No, thank you."

She sat opposite Charles, alongside Herr Berndt, who asked, "Did you find what you were looking for today, Herr Haigeron?"

"Yes, I did, although it took longer than I expected. The records in the town hall were incomplete." He looked at Frau Geyer and added, "But of course, the church keeps marriage records, too."

She said, "Of course."

He paused. Frau Geyer folded her hands in her lap and waited. Herr Berndt bit into his pastry and waited.

Charles said, "As I have told Herr Berndt, my grandfather was a journalist here in Neuberg before the First World War. His wife, my grandmother, left with their son when the war began. She lived with us when I was a child. She rarely spoke about her husband, but she kept a trunk in the attic, filled with Grandfather's diaries, copies of his newspaper columns, other clippings, and some books. I never paid any attention to any of it until a few years ago, when I retired. I suppose I had too much time on my hands. One day, I opened the trunk and read some of my grandfather's columns. I heard him speaking to me across the years. And when I began to read his diaries, he became a real person to me. I was immersed in his world. Then his words weren't enough. I studied histories of the time, fiction from that period, virtually anything I could find about Neustria and Neuberg—and the royal family."

Charles gripped the diary more tightly in his hand. He took a deep breath.

He said, "And the Terminal Project."

Herr Berndt said, "If you will forgive me, Herr Haigeron, I have told Frau Geyer about this mysterious group that your grandfather thought he had detected—the group responsible for sabotaging the Terminal."

Charles added, "And determined to overthrow the king."

Frau Geyer sighed and said, "Why should that matter now? I've told you that history has no place here."

Charles said, "But this is *your* history, Frau Geyer."

"My history?"

Charles opened his grandfather's diary to a page he had marked with a slip of yellow paper.

He said, "The last entry in Karl Haigeron's diary was written on July eighteenth. He continued to write his column for two or three weeks after that date—and then, without any notice in the newspaper, his column and his name disappeared."

Frau Geyer said, "As so many people did, during the war."

Charles said, "This is the last entry:

"I interviewed the Crown Prince today, but I cannot use the interview in my column. I fear for him. He is weary. He despairs. He says, 'We have lost our way. We have forgotten who we are. What do we celebrate? Death. Watch the crowds at Traps. They hunger for death. They applaud it. And the audiences at the Theater of Cruelty: they feel the same hunger. And they feed it. The Listeners? Narrow, bigoted, self-righteous, they speak in the voices of the dead, the angry, unforgiving dead. And the Carnival, the Carnival, where our spirit dies, our soul dies.'

"I want to comfort him, but I don't know how. He says, 'My father will not listen to me. He turns away. He shuts me out. He plays with his mistress and drinks with his generals. I warn him that he is becoming the enemy of his own people. He doesn't care.'

"The Crown Prince says, 'This is *my* country, too. This is *our* country.' He smiles at me and asks, 'It's worth saving, isn't it?' I answer, 'Yes, Your Grace, it's worth saving.'"

Charles closed the diary.

He said, "My grandfather had seen the shadows of the men who were working against the king. But he never assembled all the pieces. Because he missed the one piece that held it all together: the crown prince."

Charles watched Frau Geyer's face, but she didn't react to what he was saying.

Charles said, "The prince kept spending less and less time at the court, and more in the city. His friends were artists, writers, actors, intellectuals. Enemies of the king."

Herr Berndt said, "Perhaps he was simply a dilettante."

"No. He was seduced by them. And then he became one of them."

Herr Berndt said, "A conspirator against the king."

"How did the saboteurs know so much about the Terminal Project? How did they know when materials were going to be shipped? Where guards were stationed? Where the construction site was most vulnerable?"

"Many people knew these things," Herr Berndt said, without much conviction.

Charles asked, "Herr Berndt, what was the king's family name?"

"Löwenstein."

"Löwe—the Lion."

Herr Berndt nodded and said, "Yes, I remember those jokes you told me about: the clever carnivores. Lions, bears. That's not what I would call evidence."

Instead of answering him, Charles asked another question: "Frau Geyer, Löwenstein was your maiden name, wasn't it?"

"Yes, it was."

Charles said, "The crown prince was your grandfather."

"He was. And my grandmother was a school teacher, whom he married secretly—in Berndorf."

She smiled and said, "And I assume that you have come here to tell me all about him?"

"A prince of the royal family marries a commoner, and helps to overthrow the king. Perhaps you already know that?"

"What do you think you know? My grandfather was the leader of a group that sabotaged the Terminal Project. Yes, that's true."

"He betrayed his father."

"Yes, he did. The king killed him for that. And the king killed *your* grandfather, too, because he was one of the saboteurs."

Charles shook his head and said, "That's not true."

Frau Geyer said, "But it *is* true."

She leaned forward and said, "Herr Haigeron, what happened long ago may be a mystery to you, but is not a mystery to me. I know the story. I know everything about it. My father told me. And I told my son and daughter. Our history is not a game for you to play because you are bored. It matters to us."

She leaned back again and placed her hand over her heart.

She said, "Do you think I am ashamed of my grandfather? He was a great man. He betrayed his father because he wanted to make his country better. Is that really a betrayal? Why do you think we still preserve the ruins of the Terminal Project? Because its destruction is what we celebrate, the destruction of the old ways. My grandfather was a good man. Of course, he was a failure, too, but he tried. I'm proud of him. And you should be proud of your grandfather."

"You told me that you had never seen the name 'Haigeron' before."

She smiled and said, "I am not accustomed to freedom, Herr Haigeron. I have lived through so many difficult times that I have an instinct for secrecy.

I think that your grandmother may have suffered from the same condition. She doesn't seem to have shared any of her memories with you."

Charles said, "So my grandfather was part of the prince's group?"

"Not at first, but toward the end. He died because of it."

Charles looked down at the diary in his hand. He didn't know what to say, or how to feel.

Frau Geyer said, "You surprise me, Herr Haigeron. I didn't know that Americans had such a fondness for kings. I thought that was what your Revolutionary War was all about."

Herr Berndt said, "When the Nazis were in power, they honored the ruins of the Terminal because for them it was a symbol of the German *Volk*'s vain attempt to purge itself of the *Untermenschen* who lived here. Later, to the Communists, it represented the workers' revolt against the bourgeoisie. But for us, the meaning of the ruins was always clear: it was what remained of the first stirrings of freedom."

Frau Geyer said, "Why are you disappointed, Herr Haigeron? Did you want your story to have an unhappy ending? Isn't it better this way? You were searching for something to make your life more interesting. Now you have a brave grandfather on your family tree, eh?"

Charles remembered how empty his days and nights had been before he began to read his grandfather's journals, and how he had enjoyed the search for the truth that wasn't the truth.

He said, "I don't know."

Frau Geyer asked, "What is there to know? I guarantee you that you can never really know the past, no matter how much you study it. In my own lifetime, I have seen history rewritten so many times. I do not even trust my own memories."

Charles sat in silence for a moment. He looked out the window at the cold, gray sky of October.

Herr Berndt said, "May I presume to make a suggestion, Herr Haigeron?"

Charles shrugged.

Herr Berndt said, "All the work you have done should not go to waste. You have time on your hands? Why don't you write the true story of the Terminal Project. Perhaps we can even help you, eh?"

He looked at Frau Geyer, who hesitated and then nodded.

Charles looked at her, too.

She said, "I have some journals, some letters. Perhaps."

Frau Geyer smiled, took a deep breath and said, "My grandmother's name was Gisela—Gisela Fischer, but grandfather called her *Meine Lerche*—My Skylark."

www.ingramcontent.com/pod-product-compliance
Lightning Source LLC
Chambersburg PA
CBHW030426310726
48979CB00009B/1643/J